A FOOTBALL DREAM

By Richard Bagshaw

Illustrated by Ronnie Cashmore

2QT Limited (Publishing)

First Edition 2021

2QT Limited (Publishing)
www.2qt.co.uk

Illustrated by Ronnie Cashmore
Typesetting by Dale Rennard

Printed in Great Britain
Lightning Source UK Ltd

A CIP catalogue record for this title will be available
from the National Library
ISBN 978-1-914083-14-3

ACKNOWLEDGEMENT

To Ronnie Cashmore for bringing the book to
life with his illustrations.

DEDICATION

To my family, for the support
they gave me whilst writing the book.

CHAPTER 1

William Biggs, or Billy, as he liked to be called, was a typical nine-year-old boy who dreamt of being a footballer. Every waking moment of the day he was either watching football, talking about football, playing football, or playing football on his Nintendo. When he was asleep at night, what do you think he dreamt about? He dreamt about football. Not just any football, but him scoring the winning goal for England in the World Cup final, their first win since 1966.

When Billy and his mum were together, a typical conversation would go something like this.

'Mum, Mum, did you know that Ronaldo has won the Ballon d'Or five times, but Messi has won it six times?'

'No, Billy.'

'Mum, Mum, who do you think the best footballer ever was?'

'I'm not sure, Billy.'

'I think it was Pelé, because he was the youngest player ever to play in a team that won the World Cup.'

'Mum, Mum, who do you think is going to win the Premier League this season?'

'I don't know, Billy.'

Billy's mum, Mrs Biggs, wasn't really a football fan, but Billy would continue like this morning, noon, and night.

Billy desperately wanted to be a footballer, and he had his future football career planned out. The first team he would play for would be Birmingham Wanderers. They weren't the best team in the world, not even the best team in England, but they were Billy's favourite team, so it made sense. He would then move to Liverpool, as they were one of the best teams in England, before moving to Real Madrid for a world-record fee. He would help England win the World Cup, before moving to LA Galaxy in America for one last big season. And oh, yeah, he was also going to buy his mum a nice big house to live in, and a Range Rover to go with it. He was very generous in his dreams.

Today was exactly like any other day. Billy wanted to play football, except he was sitting on his bed looking out of his bedroom window. He turned and shouted to his mum, who was cooking dinner downstairs.

'Mum, Mum, it's raining.'

'And? What do you want me to do about it?' she replied.

'But I want to play football.'

'Well, you will have to wait until it stops. Read a book or something.'

Billy fell backwards onto his bed and looked up at his José Fernandes poster that he had strategically placed on his ceiling. José Fernandes was Billy's favourite footballer, and he had just won the Ballon d'Or the previous season.

'How can I get as good as you if I can't practise?' said Billy.

Now if this were you or me the poster wouldn't reply. After all, it was only an image of a person, not the real thing. But Billy was not you or me, and when Billy asked his poster a question it would respond.

'Billy, when I was younger, a little bit of rain would not stop me,' answered José Fernandes. 'I would be out there practising even if it were snowing to achieve my dream. Practise, practise, practise.'

Billy would often talk to his posters when he needed advice. José Fernandes gave him the inspiration he needed. He knew that José had grown up without a father, like him, and that he had been very poor, but he had still managed to achieve his dream.

José Fernandes became an image again, and Billy closed his eyes and began to imagine what it would be like to be a footballer. Billy loved to picture his future. He would be the best footballer in the world, playing alongside José Fernandes at Juventus. Juventus wasn't on his list of teams to play for, but it was the team José Fernandes played for and it was all in Billy's imagination. José Fernandes would be running down the right wing, going past one player, nutmegging another. He would get to the edge of the box, cross the ball over, and Billy would do a bicycle kick before kicking the ball into the top right-hand corner of the net.

'Goal…' The crowd would go wild, chanting Billy's name.

'There's only one Billy Biggs. One Billy Biggs. There's only one Billy Biggs.'

Now obviously Juventus is in Italy, and in Italy they speak Italian, so they wouldn't be chanting like this in English. It would be in Italian. However, this was Billy's daydream, and he couldn't speak Italian, so English would have to do. In reality it would have gone like this.

'*C'e solo un* Billy Biggs. *Un* Billy Biggs. *C'e solo un* Billy Biggs.'

By the time Billy had finished, he had scored a hat-trick and was proudly holding the match ball while being interviewed on *Match of the Day*. He was thanking José Fernandes for setting up two of his goals and, of course, his third goal was a cracking shot from the halfway line that no goalkeeper in the world, not even the England goalkeeper, could have saved. The next Ballon d'Or was coming his way.

Scoring three goals and talking to *Match of the Day* had made Billy hungry, so he opened his eyes and went downstairs to have his dinner. His mum had made him his favourite meal of sausage and mash.

The reason this was his favourite meal was not necessarily because it tasted delicious, which of course it did, but mainly because he was able to create things out of it. Billy loved to cover his dinner with gravy. He would turn the potato into a moat and use the gravy as the water surrounding it. The sausages were knights on horses jousting to win the hand of the fair maiden in distress. Or the gravy would be a swimming pool, and the potato would become a diving board. Of course, the sausage would be a person jumping off the diving board into the waiting gravy. Splash… The gravy would go everywhere, all over the table.

'Billy, stop playing with your dinner and eat it, and when you're finished make sure that every drop of that gravy is cleaned up. Do you hear me?' said Mrs Biggs.

'Yes, Mum.'
Billy took a huge bite out of his sausage. Yep, the best meal ever.

After cleaning up all the gravy, Billy's mum washed up and Billy dried. This was something that happened every night. Billy sometimes wished they had a dishwasher, but he knew they couldn't afford one, and anyway it gave them time to talk and bond.

'Mum, did you know that Birmingham Wanderers are playing at home next week?' Billy said excitedly.

'Really? That's exciting,' she responded.

'Yes, against Liverpool. Do you think they have a chance of winning the league?'

'Oh, look at that. It's stopped raining. Why don't you go outside and have a quick kickaround before you go to bed? I will finish off here,' said his mum desperately.

Billy's mum loved him, and she hoped he would achieve all his dreams one day, but sometimes talking about football wasn't high on her list of topics of conversation.

'Thanks, Mum. You're the best.'

He gave her a kiss, put on his boots, ran into the garden, and kicked the ball as hard as he could into the back of the net of his home-made goal of two pieces of wood and an old bed sheet.

'Billy Biggs scores,' he shouted excitedly, 'and the crowd goes wild.'

Billy put both his hands to his mouth and made the sound of a roaring crowd.

'Yeah…'

He did his trademark goal celebration. This was basically taking his top off and doing the dab, which involved bringing both arms to his head at an angle and pointing to the sky. He wasn't sure whether doing the dab was cool, but he was happy, and that was all that mattered.

Mrs Biggs watched him from the kitchen window and smiled. She loved to watch him, as she knew it made him so happy. She momentarily wished that his father were still around to kick a ball with him, but he wasn't and never would be. He had left when Billy was very young.

Billy didn't remember him. He sometimes thought about him, but it would pass, and he would continue doing whatever it was he was doing at the time. Billy saw his mum and waved. His mum was a wonderful mum, and she treated him the best a mum could treat a son. He couldn't be happier.

'Did you see that goal?' he shouted at her.
Mrs Biggs nodded and called him in. It was time for bed.

CHAPTER 2

The next day was Monday, and of course a school day. Billy went to Chilford Academy, which was only a five-minute walk from his home. This meant his mum could walk him to school and then catch the bus to go to work. But Billy felt he was too old to be walked to school by his mother.

'Only babies needed their mum to take them to school,' he would say.

So, as a compromise, Mrs Biggs would walk a minimum of ten paces behind him, and when he arrived at school she would leave. The most important part of this compromise was that there was absolutely no kissing goodbye. There would be a quick 'Bye,' and that was it.

So far this had worked fine, but Billy had been begging to be given a chance. His mum had finally agreed, and today was the big day. She gave him a big kiss on the doorstep and waved him goodbye. Billy walked happily and proudly to school, unaware that she was secretly following him to check he didn't do anything silly.

In 4PR, which was Billy's class, the day was known as Meditation Monday. The reason it was given this name was because Mrs Mulliner, Billy's teacher, started every Monday with a twenty-minute meditation session to get the class ready for the week. This session meant that for twenty minutes the children pictured the future they wanted. Mrs Mulliner hoped it would motivate them to work hard in their lessons. As she always said to the class,

'If you can think it...'

'You can do it,' replied the children.

They had heard this every Monday for the past three months. Mrs Mulliner was very much into self-help, ever since her pet dog Pumpkin had died and she had cried in class every day for three weeks. She began with a book entitled *I Can Make You Happy in Seven Days*.

Whenever she had a free moment in school, she would sit at her desk reading or listening to the next big thing that was going to change her life. She was currently reading a book about creating anything you want through your thoughts.

Whenever the children entered the classroom, they would be met with the smell of flowers, as Mrs Mulliner always had incense burning in the corner of the classroom before the children arrived. Obviously, for health and safety purposes, it would never be lit while the children were in the room. Billy, though, didn't mind these meditation sessions. They were the reason why he imagined himself as a professional footballer every night.

'Right, children,' said Mrs Mulliner, 'close your eyes and relax your body. I will count from twenty and you will go deeper and deeper into your meditation... Twenty, nineteen, eighteen, seventeen, sixteen, fifteen, fourteen, thirteen...'

She counted all the way down to one until finally she said, in her calmest voice,

'Relax. Picture in your mind where you see yourselves in ten years.'

This may seem quite deep for nine-year-old children, but it helped them see what they might be able to achieve. Nobody had done anything like that with them before. Most of the children enjoyed it, and their confidence grew as their dreams became bigger. They sat there with their chins in their hands and huge smiles on their faces.

Peter Queslett was imagining himself as the greatest heart surgeon in the world. He was performing a heart transplant that only he was good enough to do. Emily Chambers was prime minister of the United Kingdom. She was presiding over the country's greatest economic recovery ever. Suddenly the UK was a world leader again. Bernard Shaw was a car designer at Jaguar Land Rover, winning an award for the best new car at the annual car design awards. Missy Anderson was a detective in the New York Police Department, wearing her blue uniform and being very proud of her badge and gun. She wasn't sure how she was going to go from a little town in England to the NYPD, but Mrs Mulliner always told the children to dream big, so she did.

However, like in a lot of schools, there was always one child who spoiled things for the rest of the class. In Billy's class it happened to be a girl called Sally O'Malley. Sally was new to the school – she had only been there for three weeks – but she had already developed a reputation as a troublemaker.

Today was going to be no different. She had found a frog in her garden and decided to put it into a jar and bring it to school. While everybody else was meditating and dreaming, she decided to get the frog out of her bag and quietly tiptoed over to Mrs Mulliner's table.

Mrs Mulliner loved coffee, and every day she had a huge Americano on her table from the local cafe that she took small sips from during the remainder of the morning. Mrs Mulliner was a very nice teacher, but none of the children liked to go anywhere near her until at least after lunch, otherwise they got the smell of stale coffee when she breathed on them.

Anyway, Sally carefully took the top off the coffee cup and placed the frog inside. By now the coffee was quite cool, so the frog wasn't harmed at all. Sally carefully placed the lid back on the coffee and crept back to her seat. She closed her eyes and pretended to meditate.

The alarm began to ring on Mrs Mulliner's clock, and everybody began to open their eyes. Billy was disappointed because he was just about to score a goal for Birmingham Wanderers.

'How wonderful was that? I hope all your dreams come true,' said Mrs Mulliner, with the biggest smile on her face.

What she hadn't told the children was that while in meditation she was visualising herself retired and lying on a warm beach in Dubai. While still thinking about that she took a deep breath and yawned, as meditating had made her quite drowsy, before she reached for her coffee.

As she brought the coffee cup to her lips, Sally sat forward on her chair and had the most devious expression on her face. Mrs Mulliner opened her mouth and poured the coffee down her throat.

'Mmm… There is nothing better than a cup of coffee in the morning.'
She placed the coffee cup on the table and stood up.

'Right, children. Today we are going to begin with maths and multiplying fractions.'

She turned to the whiteboard and brought up her beautifully prepared PowerPoint presentation, which she was going to use to teach the children today's subjects. What she didn't see as she turned around was the sudden movement of her coffee cup. Some of the children saw it but momentarily didn't believe their eyes, so they waited to see if it moved again. And of course it did. Suddenly there was the sound of mumbling in the classroom, as the children who had seen it move began nudging the other children to make them aware of what was happening. The cup moved again.

'What is all this noise, children? Silence, please. You know how to behave in my class by now. You have been here long enough,' said Mrs Mulliner, with annoyance in her voice.

Emily Chambers, the complete opposite of Sally O'Malley, as she was the most perfect student in the class, put her hand up and said,

'Miss.'

Mrs Mulliner turned around again in frustration and snapped,

'Yes, Emily?'

'Miss, your cup is moving,' Emily replied.

'Don't be silly, Emily. This is so unlike you to join in with the silliness of the class.'

'I'm not lying, Mrs Mulliner. Your coffee cup is moving.'

Mrs Mulliner stopped and looked over the top of her glasses, which were resting on the end of her nose, at her coffee cup. The children all leant forward on their chairs in anticipation of the coffee cup moving again. The class became quiet as Sally tried her hardest not to burst into the biggest laugh ever.

Then suddenly the cup moved and fell over, and Mrs Mulliner and the children screeched from the shock of it all. The coffee began to leak out of the side of the lid of the cup, as Mrs Mulliner pushed it with a very long metre ruler. She pushed it once more, and as she did so, the lid of the cup fell off and out jumped the frog.

'Ribbit,' it said.

The whole class jumped and squealed as the huge green frog jumped off the table onto the floor and hopped around the classroom.

'Ribbit, ribbit,' said the frog again. The children jumped onto their chairs, Mrs Mulliner jumped onto her chair, and everyone began to scream. Just as the screams got really loud the head teacher, Mr Hussain, who had been walking past, opened the door to the classroom and stepped inside with a look of anger on his face and shouted,

'What is the meaning of all this noise?'

'A frog, Headmaster … in my coffee … on the floor,' cried Mrs Mulliner, as she pointed in the direction that it had hopped away in.

'A frog … where?'

'There,' shouted the children.

Mr Hussain saw the frog hopping around the classroom floor and went over and picked it up. Billy noticed that Mr Hussain had unusually large hands. In his mind they looked like the size of the foam hands that are popular at sports games. They were not really that big, but they were bigger than the average person's hands. They were so big that the frog could no longer be seen, and it was a big frog. Nobody seemed to know why Mr Hussain's hands were so big. They just were.

'Would somebody like to explain to me what a frog is doing on the floor in one of my classrooms?' He looked at Mrs Mulliner. 'Really, I expect more from you.'

Mrs Mulliner jumped down from her chair and began composing herself, pulling down her skirt and brushing back her long brown hair with her hands.

'Yes, Headmaster. I am very sorry, Headmaster.'

Mr Hussain turned back to the children and shouted,

'Well, come on.'

Mr Hussain liked to shout. It was the only way he knew how to get children to understand just how upset he was. He was a very young headmaster at only twenty-nine years of age. He hadn't taught for very long before heading up the promotional ladder to headmaster, so he hadn't learnt the many different techniques of persuasion that good teachers learn over time.

Emily, as you would expect, began to explain in great detail exactly what had happened.

'So how did a frog get into Mrs Mulliner's coffee? It didn't just hop in there by itself.'

He turned to Mrs Mulliner.

'You didn't ask for a frog in your coffee, did you? Just to be clear.'

'No, Headmaster.'

The children laughed, as they thought Mr Hussain was making a joke.

'Quiet,' he shouted at them again. 'So, is anybody going to own up?'

Everybody looked at everybody else, until finally all eyes were staring at Sally. She looked around and in the most innocent of responses, as if butter wouldn't melt in her mouth, she said,

'I didn't do it. Why do I always get the blame?'

'Well, somebody did it, and the culprit has thirty seconds to own up or everybody will be in detention tonight,' Mr Hussain said firmly.

The class went silent as everybody's eyes went from watching the seconds tick by on the clock to looking at the potential suspects in the class. They went first to Sally, then to Jason Jackson, who had a reputation of doing practical jokes on people, before finally looking at Evan Johnson, who was the class bully.

'Fifteen seconds to go,' said a very distressed Mr Hussain.

'Come on, Sally, own up. We know it's you… I am not having detention for something I didn't do,' cried a very upset Malcolm Jacobs, Billy's best friend.

'Five seconds, four seconds, three seconds, two seconds, one second… Right. I want to see everybody, and I mean everybody, back in here at three thirty this afternoon,' said Mr Hussain.

There was a big groan in the classroom.

'I will inform all your parents why you will be staying tonight, and I am sure they will all be very disappointed about the events that have happened this morning. Mrs Mulliner, can I see you outside?'

Mr Hussain turned and left the classroom, and Mrs Mulliner quietly followed. The class watched as Mr Hussain talked to her. They could see her nodding as his finger began pointing in the direction of the class. Finally, she returned to the classroom, sat down on her chair, and placed her head in her hands. The children stayed dead silent, then suddenly a sobbing could be head coming from her direction. The children began looking at each other, unsure of what they should do. Then Billy decided to ask Mrs Mulliner a question.

'Are you OK, miss?'

After a moment Mrs Mulliner looked up. A tear trickled down her cheek. She wiped it away and quietly replied,

'Yes, I am fine. I am just being a little silly, that's all.'

Billy looked over at Sally, as he had his suspicions that it was her too. He just knew that she was the cause of it all, and she even looked a little upset at what had occurred. Mrs Mulliner stood up and composed herself.

'Right now, where were we? Oh, yes, multiplying fractions.'

CHAPTER 3

Finally, the lunch bell rang, and the children all left the classroom and went into the playground. Billy and Malcolm ran to the grassy area to start their daily game of football, but they were met by Mr Jenkins the PE teacher. Mr Jenkins was dressed, as usual, in his bright red tracksuit. If he had not been wearing a tracksuit you would never suspect that he was in fact a PE teacher. Normally when you think of a PE teacher you would perhaps imagine an athletic figure, somebody who enjoys playing sports, and especially likes fitness, which is obviously an important aspect of the job.

Take a moment to think about what your PE teacher looks like. Mr Jenkins didn't look like that at all. He looked like he hadn't played any sport for a very long time. His athletic figure had been replaced by a huge beach ball of a tummy that bounced around whenever he walked. His tracksuit top was always just a little bit too small and rested on the top of his tummy rather than covered it, so his belly button was always on show. When the children were having their lesson they would be doing all the hard work, while he watched, eating a packet of salt and vinegar crisps.

'Stop,' he said.

Mr Jenkins attached a piece of paper to the noticeboard next to the football pitch. He looked like he was going to enjoy what he was about to share with the children.

'Read this, please,' he said, with a grin on his face.

Malcolm and the other children who were arriving began reading the notice that Mr Jenkins had prepared. Billy decided to read it out loud.

Due to the sheer number of children who play football each break, and the fact that the younger children never get the opportunity to play, I have created a timetable that everybody must follow. This will enable each year group to play football every week.

Each day will be allocated to a particular year: Mondays Years 1 and 2, Tuesdays Year 3, Wednesdays Year 4, Thursdays Year 5 and Fridays Year 6. You are not allowed on the field unless it is your allocated day. Anybody who doesn't adhere to these rules will be banned for the rest of the year.

Billy turned to Mr Jenkins.

'We can't play until Wednesday, and then only once a week. That is so unfair.'

'That is so unfair,' repeated Mr Jenkins, in what he considered a very childish voice. 'Well, it is fair. We had to do something so everybody could have a chance to play, and this was the best option for everybody. If you are in Years 1 and 2 you can go and play on the field now. If not, off you go. Bye-bye.'

Mr Jenkins waved in the direction of the older children who were not playing. There was a cheer from the Years 1 and 2 children as they ran off and began their game, and a groan from the rest of the children whose turn it was another day. Billy and Malcolm began to walk away.

'I can't believe we can't play football until Wednesday. That's two whole days away,' complained Billy.

'No, Mr Jenkins said we were not allowed on the field. We can still play football. It will just have to be with a tennis ball, since that is all that's left,' said Malcolm, who was very proud of himself for thinking of a way around the new rules.

Malcolm got a tennis ball and passed it to Billy, who tried to kick it but missed it and watched as it trickled past him.

'How am I meant to play football with a tennis ball? It's too small. I bet José Fernandes never had to kick a tennis ball around,' said an angry Billy.

'My dad said that in Brazil the people are very poor, and they can't afford footballs, so they play with tennis balls. My dad said that is why they are the best team in the world and always have the best footballers. My dad said that if you can play football with a tennis ball, then you can play football with anything.'

At that, Malcolm kicked the tennis ball in the air and proceeded to keep the ball up using both his left foot and his right foot. The ball didn't touch the ground until after Malcolm had kept it up five times.

'Give me a go,' said an eager Billy.

Billy kicked the ball up with his right foot and went to kick it again, but he missed it. He tried again but missed it again.

'This is stupid… It's called football, not tennisball.'

Billy then went to kick the ball as hard as he could, but it just trickled away back to Malcolm. Billy stormed off in a huff. He went to sit on the grass to watch the younger children play football and stayed there until the bell rang for the end of playtime.

After outdoor play it was assembly, so all the children lined up and made their way into the assembly hall. They sat down in their rows, then Mr Hussain stood up to talk to the children.

'Today, children, we have some very special and some very exciting news to share with you. I have just received a phone call from Birmingham Wanderers, who have informed me that on Wednesday Diego Francesco, their exciting new Italian striker, will be coming to the school to talk to you all.'

There was an excited cheer from the children. Mr Hussain continued,

'He will be sharing with you some news about a new initiative that Birmingham Wanderers are setting up. All I can say is that it is very exciting, and Mr Jenkins has told me that he can't wait to get started on it. We are looking for one volunteer—'

All the children put their hands up and started shouting,

'Me … me … me.'

'Put your hands down and listen, please. We are looking for one volunteer to show Mr Francesco around the school.' Mr Hussain held up a box for the children to see. 'Mr Jenkins has decided that if you are interested you can put your name in this box, and we will draw the name of the volunteer first thing in the morning.'

This was the last thing that Billy heard during the assembly and possibly for the remainder of the day. He began to daydream about showing Diego Francesco around the school. Diego Francesco was not just any player. He was the record signing from last summer at Birmingham Wanderers. And he was the man who had so far scored five goals in his first nine games, the man who Billy aimed to replace on the right wing one day, before moving to Liverpool.

Billy couldn't contain his excitement any longer. He put his hand up, which was quite unusual in an assembly. Mr Hussain looked at Billy and frowned.

'I hope this is important,' he said.

'It is, sir,' Billy replied.

'Well, go on, then.'

'Sir, you have got to let me show Diego Francesco around. He is my favourite player, and I can discuss football with him all day. It is my destiny.'

Mr Hussain smiled. The other children began to giggle. Billy became a little embarrassed.

'It is your destiny, is it, Billy? We all know about your passion for football,' said Mr Hussain. 'It is legendary around here. But, like I said, put your name in the box and you will have just as much chance as anybody else.'

'Yes, sir.'

The children laughed again.

'Right. Let's move on.'

One of the children in Year 6 nudged Billy in the back and mimicked,

'It is my destiny,' in his silliest voice.

Billy became embarrassed again, but pretended that he didn't care.

CHAPTER 4

Lunchtime finally arrived, and Billy rushed to the cafeteria, so that he could finish his food quickly, and then go and put his name in the box. He reached the counter and looked at all the delicious food that was on offer … except that as usual the food looked like it had been dropped on the floor, trodden on, and put in some kind of red liquid before being served. The smell was disgusting as well, as if somebody had vomited and mixed it in the food. Billy looked at the dinner lady, Mrs Higgins, and said with a sarcastic smile,

'Delicious, as usual. And that aroma … mmm… I can't quite place it. I am sure I have smelt it somewhere before. Do you know what it is?'

The dinner lady looked at Billy and growled,

'Do you want it or what?'

'Of course. How could I resist such a fine meal?'

The dinner lady threw it onto Billy's tray, accidentally on purpose spraying some of it on Billy's face. She smiled and showed her stained yellow teeth covered in red lipstick, as she watched a trickle of red goo slither down Billy's face. He wiped it off and tasted it.

'Mmm, lovely. Pleasure, as usual. I can see you have already partaken of the meal, as you still have some of it on your teeth,' said Billy.

'What are you talking about? I wouldn't eat this tripe. In fact, I wouldn't risk giving it to a dog. I know what goes into it,' the dinner lady said, and smirked.

'I must have been mistaken.'

The dinner lady grunted, and Billy made his way to the table. He pinched his nose, so he didn't have to smell the food, and slowly forced it into his mouth. Most people would probably not have managed even one mouthful, but Billy was quite peckish and needed something to get him through the remainder of the day.

He began to chew. The vomit-like smell wasn't misleading, because as he chewed Billy realised that the food also tasted like vomit. He spat it out back onto the tray and drank his glass of water in one go.

'That was disgusting,' he said to himself.

Billy stood up, ready to go and throw the remainder in the bin, when Mr Jenkins stopped him.

'Where do you think you're going?'

'I've finished, sir,' replied Billy, wincing as his tongue managed to find a piece of food lodged between his teeth.

'I don't think so. You are not leaving until every last piece has gone off your tray.'

'But sir, it's disgusting.'

'No, it isn't. I have just finished mine and it was delicious. Now sit down.'

Mr Jenkins hadn't really eaten the food. He had learnt a long time ago never to eat the school meals, so every day he brought in some leftovers from his dinner the night before. Today he had leftover pepperoni pizza. When he had to lie to Billy, he imagined the pizza so that he was more convincing. His mouth became moist, and he began to drool as he thought about the taste. Billy sat back down and looked at his food.

'I'll be watching you, Billy,' said a smirking Mr Jenkins.

He turned away, but then stopped and looked back at Billy. He then placed his index and middle finger to his eyes and then pointed them at him.

'Watching you,' he repeated.

Billy couldn't face eating his food. The smell, the taste, the look… It was just not something that he could face eating at all. So he undid the zip of the corner pocket in his bag and started spooning it in. He looked around to make sure nobody was looking, then poured the remainder in too. He had zipped up the bag when Mr Jenkins looked at him again, so he continued to pretend eating to look authentic. He held up the spoon and said,

'Yummy.'

Billy put his tray away and then left the canteen, unaware that his food was leaking from his bag and leaving a trail behind him. He rushed to put his name inside the box, which had been placed outside Mr Hussain's office.

As he left, Mrs Perkins, Mr Hussain's secretary, was returning to her desk after having her lunch. She did not see the trail of food on the floor, and as you might expect, trod on the food, slipped, and completed a somersault in the air before landing bottom first on the floor.

Billy saw what had happened and felt sorry for her. However, so that he didn't get into any more trouble today, he decided to run to the bathroom and clean out his bag, rather than help her. It was not the best decision Billy could have made in those circumstances, but luckily Mrs Perkins didn't hurt herself and managed to get back to her desk in one piece. She looked around her to make sure that nobody saw her gymnastics, as she felt quite embarrassed about falling over and landing on her bottom.

Unbeknown to Billy and the rest of the school, Sally had been hatching a plan to ensure she would win the competition. Instead of having her lunch – and, to be honest, she didn't miss much – she spent her time writing her name down on lots of pieces of paper. She was determined to win, and by the time she had finished she had written her name down two hundred and twenty-seven times.

She went to Mr Hussain's office and made sure that nobody was around before placing her pieces of paper in the box. As she placed the last one in, Mr Hussain's door opened, and he stepped out.

'Oh, hello, Sally. Are you entering the competition?' he asked.

'Yes, sir.'

'Good. The more the merrier … but I didn't know you liked football.'

'I don't, sir, but I thought it would be an honour showing a guest around the school,' she replied in her most sarcastic voice that teachers, for some reason, tended to hear as genuine honesty.

'That's very thoughtful of you. Now off you go, back to class. You're going to be late.'

Sally walked away with a venomous smile on her face. She was telling the truth when she told Mr Hussain that she didn't like football, but she hated lessons even more. Spending time out of the classroom showing Diego around was the perfect excuse to not go to them. However, her plan would only work if Mr Hussain didn't check the names for any cheating. Unfortunately, Mr Hussain was a very trusting headteacher, so he wouldn't be likely to.

Detention that afternoon was deadly boring, which is how it should be when children have misbehaved in school. The children were told to sit quietly and read their books for an hour. Billy began reading his football book about the world's best goals. He imagined doing every kick that was described in it.

Every now and then a child would look at Sally, but Sally didn't care. In her mind, having detention was worth every minute for the ten minutes of fun they had had that morning.

Emily complained to Mr Hussain that she didn't deserve it because she had never misbehaved in her life, and that it was totally unfair. Mr Hussain explained again the reason why the whole class was there and hoped that the culprit would still own up sooner rather than later, but Sally didn't. All the children knew it was her, as she was the cause of all the chaos in their class, but nobody dared say anything.

That evening went really slowly for Billy. He spent some of the evening playing FIFA 21 on his Nintendo Switch, he practised scoring goals in the garden, and he pictured meeting Diego. What he was imagining went something like this…

After his name was pulled out as the winner, everybody in assembly, both teachers and children, started cheering his name because they were so glad that he had won.

Then Diego arrived and met Billy. Diego told him he was his greatest fan because he had heard how fantastic he was at football, and asked if they could have a quick kickaround. Billy showed Diego his skills and they became the best of friends. Well, who wouldn't want to be the best of friends with the world's greatest footballer, Billy Biggs?

Billy might have been the one chosen to meet Diego Francesco if Sally hadn't cheated and put her name in the box two hundred and twenty-seven times. Unfortunately, she had, so little did he know that he had absolutely no chance of being the one to show him around. Buying a National Lottery ticket possibly offered a better chance of winning than Billy had of winning this competition, but even so he went to sleep dreaming of meeting his hero.

CHAPTER 5

The next day the children hurried to school full of anticipation, hoping that their name would be the chosen one. Billy arrived first in class and discovered that Mrs Mulliner was absent. Today they had a supply teacher called Mr Baxter instead. When Mr Baxter arrived at a new school, he liked to let the children know who was in charge, and today was no different.

'Good morning, class. My name is Mr Baxter, and I will be your teacher for today. Now it seems that the reason I am here today is because this class caused Mrs Mulliner to have a bit of a confidence crisis.'

The class sat motionless as they stared at Mr Baxter, when suddenly Emily put her hand up.

'Put your hand down. I am talking,' said an annoyed Mr Baxter.

Emily had never been spoken to that way before by a teacher. She had always been the perfect student, getting top marks in all class tests, and had always been the teacher's favourite. She was the kind of student that teachers wished they had a class full of, but instead they seemed to get more Sally O'Malleys than Emily Chambers. In fact, she was so unprepared for that kind of response that she looked like she was going to cry.

'Let's get one thing sorted now. I am the teacher, which means that I talk and you listen. Only when I ask for a response do I expect to see hands go up. I do not expect any shouting out, and I certainly don't expect to hear any talking.'

Mr Baxter was the kind of teacher who was not good enough to be employed by a school, which is why he was a supply teacher. This is not meant to dismiss supply teachers. Most are very good and have their own reasons why they decide to become supply teachers, but Mr Baxter was different. His knowledge of the school subjects was excellent, and he knew how to teach. It was just that he came across as a little... Well, it's best to just say that children were not his favourite kind of people.

This begs the question of why he went into teaching in the first place. The answer was quite simple. When he was younger, he always wanted to be famous. He didn't care how or what he did to be famous. He just craved the limelight. He always wanted to walk down the street, and know that everybody knew his name, wanted his autograph, and wanted their photograph taken with him.

However, there was one small problem. He didn't really have any talent for anything. He couldn't sing, and in fact he was tone-deaf. When he auditioned for the well-known talent contest, *Britain Can Sing*, the judges couldn't stop laughing because they thought he was a prank audition. Nor could he act. He sounded like a robot when he read the lines. The closest he came to being an actor was as Boy number 4 in a commercial, and even then, he was only on the screen for two seconds.

He couldn't play any sport very well, and... Quite frankly, he was boring, so reality TV shows were not exactly begging for him to appear on their programmes. That is why he ended up being a teacher. It wasn't because he loved children or even had a passion for teaching. No. He wanted the long holidays. He had thought to himself that if he couldn't have the fame or the fortune, he would at least have a lot of free time. That is how he ended up at Billy's school, a miserable single man, counting the days until the next school holiday – which, as everyone knows, is never that far away when you're a teacher.

The children were not prepared for this kind of attitude. After all, Mrs Mulliner was so nice and caring. But they sat, and they listened … and listened … and listened, until their poor heads were nearly drooping down to the floor from boredom.

When Mr Jenkins knocked on the door it was a welcome relief for everybody.

'Good morning. Sorry to disturb you, but it is assembly time, and we are waiting.'

'I am so sorry. I didn't know,' replied Mr Baxter, with a different, more polite tone than the one he used with the children.

Mr Jenkins left, and Mr Baxter became the horrid man that he had been previously.

'Why didn't anybody tell me you had assembly this morning?' he snapped. 'Making me look like a fool.'

Billy whispered to Malcolm,

'Er … because you told us not to talk.'

'Quickly, line up at the door,' Mr Baxter said sternly.

They quietly walked into assembly, with Mr Hussain waiting on the stage for them. They seemed to have a lot of assemblies at Chilford Academy, and this week was no different.

'Ah, I am so glad you have finally decided to join us,' Mr Hussain said in a somewhat sarcastic manner. 'Today is the big day,' he continued to the rest of the children. 'I am sure you are all interested in finding out who the lucky winner is, who will show Diego Francesco around the school tomorrow.'

There was a huge noise as the children began talking to their friends with an excited anticipation.

'Quiet, please. Well, without further ado… Mr Jenkins, if you would like to step forward and be so kind and pull out the winning name…'

Mr Jenkins stood up and slowly walked over to where the box was. He put his hand in and pulled out a piece of paper.

Billy, along with so many of the other children, had his fingers crossed and was chanting to himself,

'Please let it be me. Please let it be me.'

Mr Jenkins opened the piece of paper and looked at the name.

'Interesting,' he said. 'The person who is going to be showing the Birmingham Wanderers star Diego Francesco around the school tomorrow is … ta-dah … Sally O'Malley.'

The rest of the children groaned as Sally shouted,

'Yes.' She stood up and bowed to the rest of the children.

'Thank you, thank you. I would just like to thank Mr Jenkins for pulling my name out of the box and for Mr Hussain for giving me this great opportunity. Thank you, thank you. You can all love me now.'

'OK, that is enough, Sally. Sit down,' Mr Jenkins said, giggling.

Billy looked at Malcolm and whispered angrily,

'I can't believe she won... She doesn't even like football.'

'Thank you, Mr Jenkins, and well done to Sally. You have a very important day ahead of you tomorrow,' said Mr Hussain.

As the children began leaving the hall, Billy whispered to Malcolm,

'There is something not right about this. How can Sally, out of all of us, be the one who was picked?'

'There is nothing we can do about it now,' replied Malcolm.

'I want to check that box. She must have tampered with it,' said a frustrated Billy.

'What you want to do?'

'Let's wait outside until everybody leaves and have a look.'

So, Billy and Malcolm waited outside the assembly hall, and, when everybody had left, they crept back in and emptied the names out of the box. Billy picked out a piece of paper and read it.

'*Sally O'Malley.*'

Malcolm picked one out and saw the name on it and read it to Billy.

'Look. *Sally O'Malley*. I can't believe it. That's why she won. She cheated.'

'We have got to do something about this,' said an angry Billy. 'First we get detention, and now this.'

Malcolm continued picking out names.

'*Sally O'Malley, Sally O'Malley*. What shall we do? Tell Mr Hussain?'

'No. We have got to do something that will embarrass her in front of everyone. It has to be good.'

Now when Malcolm had completed his education, he wanted to be a chef. Every Monday, when they all did their imagination exercises, Malcolm closed his eyes and saw himself as a world-famous chef, with a restaurant that had three Michelin stars, which are of course only given to the very best restaurants.

This ambition of Malcolm's led to an idea that was intended to be so embarrassing for Sally that he hoped it would go down in history at their school, and that future generations of children would talk about it for a very long time. Malcolm was going to enjoy putting his plan into action.

What he and Billy were going to do was not the right response, because you should never retaliate like they were planning to do. Telling Mr Hussain would have been the right thing to do. But they were out for revenge.

After school Malcolm went home and began making some scones, while Billy went to the pharmacy to buy some laxatives.

When buying any type of medicine, it is important to follow the instructions on the box exactly. However, Billy and Malcolm did not. They mashed up all the laxative tablets and sprinkled them into one of the scones. If they had read the instructions, they would have seen that a maximum of three laxatives should be taken in a twenty-four-hour period. But they mashed up twelve. So this was a very special scone, and in fact this scone was being made especially for Sally.

So that they didn't confuse this scone with the others, they placed a cherry on top of it. They then made enough scones for the whole of the class.

CHAPTER 6

The next day, Malcolm arrived at school with his scones. Mrs Mulliner was still absent, and so Mr Baxter was their teacher again. All the children groaned as they walked into the classroom and saw him. Malcolm wasn't sure whether his idea was going to work, as Mr Baxter didn't seem like the kind of person who would allow this sort of nice touch in his class. He took the scones to him anyway, as he had to try and continue with his plan, and said,

'Mr Baxter, would it be OK if I gave everybody a scone to try? I have a cooking competition I'd like to enter, and I would appreciate some feedback on them.'

Mr Baxter looked at the scones and groaned,

'Why would I let you do that?'

'Because I have made one for you,' replied Malcolm, handing him a scone with a huge, innocent smile on his face.

Mr Baxter took a bite out of it, and for one small moment he looked like he had a hint of pleasure on his face. Only for a short moment, though, as it soon passed. Mr Baxter looked at Malcolm. Malcolm looked at Mr Baxter. Billy was watching them with anticipation.

'Go on, then, but don't make this a habit. It is only going to happen this once,' said Mr Baxter.

Malcolm then proceeded to give each child in the class one scone. Billy and Malcolm were eating theirs, while at the same time watching Sally eating hers.

Sally took a small bite out of her scone. A pleasant look appeared on her face, and she then proceeded to gobble it down in almost one go. The cherry was thrown in the bin, as she detested anything healthy. Billy and Malcolm looked at each other and smiled.

At that moment Mr Hussain walked into the classroom.

'Could I have Sally, please, Mr Baxter?'

'Of course. Off you go, Sally, and good luck.'

Sally looked at Billy and put her right hand to her forehead with her index finger and thumb, making an L shape.

'Loser,' she said.

The look on her face showed Billy that she thought she had beaten him. Billy just looked back at her and smiled.

All the children went into the hall, so they could hear the announcement that Diego Francesco was going to make. Sally was sitting on the stage next to him with a huge grin from ear to ear. Mr Hussain arrived and introduced Diego to the children and some of the children began to chant,

'Diego, Diego, Diego…'

At that moment, just as he was about to begin talking, Sally began fidgeting on her chair. She heard her stomach rumble, along with feeling a slight pain. Her stomach began making a groaning sound. She stood up for a second and looked like she was about to run off the stage, but changed her mind and sat back down. She held her stomach again and stood up. Her face changed colour and she began to look pale. Some children began noticing what Sally was doing and began nudging their friends, so they could watch the events unfold. Sally began to panic.

'Mr Hussain, I am not feeling very well. I need to go to the bathroom,' said a very anxious Sally.

Mr Hussain stopped and looked at Diego.

'I am very sorry about this,' he said, then said to Sally,

'Can it not wait?'

'I need to go now, sir.'

Sally didn't wait for Mr Hussain's acknowledgement and began walking to the edge of the stage, holding her stomach and clenching her bottom. But it was too late. A loud noise that could only be described as a foghorn erupted from her bottom. The children began to laugh as another foghorn sound filled the assembly hall.

Mr Hussain and Diego Francesco began to pull disgusted faces and held their noses as a nasty smell began making its way towards them. Suddenly everybody went quiet as they saw a brown and runny gooey liquid, which must have come from Sally, create a small puddle on the stage. Sally looked at what she had done, then looked at the children staring at her as she screamed,

'I want my mummy.'

There was a moment of silence before the children in the audience broke into laughter. Sally jumped off the stage and ran out of the assembly hall. Unfortunately, the children in Year 1 who were sitting at the front of the hall and near the incident could smell Sally's accident. Some children began to cry, while others started to feel sick. Even Diego, who was by now standing on the stage and looking very confused about what he had just witnessed, felt a little sick too.

'Teachers, please take your children back to the classroom,' said Mr Hussain, before ushering Diego away with him in the opposite direction of the puddle.

Billy and Malcolm sat watching with their arms crossed and smiles on their faces, assessing what they had done. They felt it was a good comeuppance for everything Sally had done. The rest was unfortunate and unforeseen.

Just as 4PR arrived back in the classroom, the school nurse came in.

'Sir, Sally O'Malley is not feeling very well, so she is going home.'

The class gave a little snigger.

'Thank you for letting me know,' replied Mr Baxter. 'What a strange turn of events ... such a shame it had to happen on such an important day for her.'

At that moment Mr Hussain came into the classroom and asked,

'Could I see Billy for a moment, please?'

Billy stood up and followed Mr Hussain out of the classroom.

'Billy, after Sally's unfortunate accident, I was hoping you would take her place and show Diego around the school.'

'Would I? Yes, sir.' He stopped for a moment and asked, 'Sir, would it be possible for Malcolm to help show him around too? He is a big fan of Diego's and my best friend.'

'OK, just this once.'

'Thank you, sir.'

Billy went back into the classroom and told Malcolm. After all, Billy wouldn't be in this lucky position if it hadn't been for Malcolm's master plan and fine culinary skills.

They followed Mr Hussain to his office. He opened the door, and there sitting in a chair sipping tea, was the world-famous Diego Francesco. They ran over to him.

'I am your biggest fan. I know everything about you and love you so much,' cried Billy.

'It is an honour to meet you. I love you too,' said Malcolm.

They stood next to Diego and then continued to stare at him while Mr Hussain explained that they would give him a guided tour of the school.

'I will arrange for the whole school to come to assembly again in one hour, and hopefully this time it will pass without any incidents,' said Mr Hussain.

Billy and Malcolm sniggered. They left the office and began showing Diego around the school.

'Do you like scones?' asked Malcolm.

'Scones, what are these scones?' asked Diego.

Diego was Italian, so he hadn't heard of the British delicacy that is the scone.

'There you go. Try this. I made it for you.'

Diego looked at it for a moment, sniffed it and then placed his tongue on it hesitantly.

'It's like a cake,' Billy said to reassure him.

Diego took a bite out of the scone and his face changed to an expression of exhilaration.

'It is like nothing I have ever tasted. Why has nobody given me this to try before? It is a delicious sensation in my mouth.'

'You should try it with jam and cream,' said Malcolm, laughing.

Diego then finished the scone in seconds while Malcolm watched with great satisfaction as his creation was demolished by his idol.

'Do you have any more?' asked Diego.

'No, sorry, just the one,' replied Malcolm.

'It was delicious,' said Diego.

Billy and Malcolm showed Diego around the school until finally they reached the sports field.

'Can we have a kickaround?' asked Billy.

'Sure, why not?' replied Diego.

'Excellent. I'll get a ball.'

Billy and Diego proceeded to pass the ball around. Billy kicked it up in the air and asked,

'Was that good?'

Diego replied,

'*Si*,' which is Italian for 'Yes'.

Billy passed the ball to Diego and asked again,

'Was that good?'

Diego replied,

'*Si*, but hit the ball on the side. Yes,' he said, while pointing to his foot, 'and look in the direction you are passing. It will be more accurate. *Si*, I mean yes.'

At this stage Malcolm started to feel a little left out, as Billy was taking up all Diego's time. Malcolm loved football too, but not as much as Billy. He was fine with them kicking the ball around, but he was just getting a little bored. He looked at his watch and saw what time it was.

'We need to get to the hall. It's assembly time.'

'Oh, just five more minutes,' said Billy.

'We need to go,' said Malcolm.

On the way to the assembly hall Billy looked at Diego, as he had decided to ask him something. He knew that he might not have the chance after assembly, so he was busy building up the courage. Finally he managed to spit it out.

'You know, we are having meatballs and spaghetti for dinner tonight. That is an Italian dish, isn't it?'

'*Si* … my favourite,' replied Diego.

'Well, I was wondering if you would like to come for dinner. It's only me and my mum, and it would be nice to have a guest.'

'Oh, I don't know. I am not sure your mama would appreciate my just turning up.'

'She won't mind, honestly, and she is a good cook. The best.'

'OK. I haven't had a proper homecooked meal since coming here,' replied Diego. 'But only if you're sure.'

'No problem.'

Billy whispered,

'Yes,' to himself before doing a little jig, and typed his address into Diego's phone. By the time they got to the assembly hall everybody was waiting for them.

Billy looked at Mr Hussain and whispered,

'Sorry,' to him.

Then Diego stood up in front of the school and shared the news from a prepared written speech.

'It is with great pleasure that I am here today. I have made some great friends,' he said, as he turned and looked at Billy and Malcolm, 'and I have been made to feel very special. Birmingham Wanderers asked me to come today to give you some exciting news. Football in schools does not happen as often as it used to, so we have decided to set up a cup competition, the Birmingham Wanderers Shield, where ten schools will compete in two leagues of five. The winner of each league will play each other at our home ground, Valley Park, before the last game of the season against Manchester United.'

An excited rumble came from the children. A huge grin came over Billy and Malcolm's faces as Diego continued.

'Your school has been chosen to take part in the under tens division. If you get through to the final you will need to first play ten games in the league, and then the eleventh game will be the final. Thank you for listening, and goodbye.'

The children cheered as Diego left the stage. Mr Jenkins then came to the front and explained what they needed to do if they wanted to participate and register for the team. He was waving a list and showed it to the children, saying,

'Those children interested will need to put their names down on this list, which will be outside my office. Our first game is next Wednesday, so the list will be taken down by the end of today.'

When the classes were dismissed, Billy and Malcolm rushed off the stage and went straight to Mr Jenkins's office and put their names down as number one and two respectively. They jumped up and down and shouted together,

'Valley Park, Valley Park.'

Billy couldn't wait to get home that afternoon. He rushed into the house and barged into the living room and announced to his mum that they would be having a guest for dinner and that they needed to have meatballs and spaghetti.

'You should have asked before inviting anybody, Billy. Who is it?

'Diego Francesco.'

'Who?'

'The Birmingham Wanderers player.'

'Stop being silly, Billy. Why would he come here for dinner?'

Billy explained to her what had happened at school that day and how he had got to show Diego around, play football with him, and that he had asked him to come. Billy's mum screamed and said,

'I've got to go and have a shower and wash my hair.'

At that she ran upstairs and began singing a song, which started with the line,

'There's only one Diego Francesco.'

She had been used to hearing Billy sing football songs for years and had had to listen to them over and over again, and had subconsciously learnt the words.

After her shower Billy's mum came back downstairs looking very pretty. She was wearing her best dress, she had let her long brown hair flow over her shoulders – it would usually be in a ponytail – and was wearing make-up.

'What are you dressed like that for?' asked Billy, in a very suspicious way.

'Just trying to look nice for our guest, Billy.'

'Oh, but couldn't you just dress normally?' he said.

'Sometimes it's nice to make an effort.'

Billy's mum began cooking the meatballs and spaghetti. At seven o'clock exactly the doorbell rang, and Billy ran to open it. Mrs Biggs looked in the mirror to check she still looked good before Billy brought him into the dining room.

'Mrs Biggs, I hope I am not inconveniencing you by coming this evening,' said a concerned Diego.

'No, not at all. It's nice to have a guest. It's usually just Billy and me.'

'Billy said your spaghetti and meatballs are delicious. I have been looking forward to dinner since he invited me.'

'Please take a seat. We're almost ready.'

Billy watched as Diego sat down, and just stared at him. He wanted to remember everything about the night. He felt a little overwhelmed by having a famous footballer sitting at his dining table. It took him a moment to realise it was really happening. Then he said,

'I wasn't sure you would come.'

'I said I would, and it important to me to keep my word. I am lucky enough to be in position of responsibility and I don't like letting people down. If you keep your word people respect you.'

Unbeknown to them, a neighbour had recognised Diego and had seen him entering the house. The neighbour called a local newspaper and told them what he had seen. This led to a few newspaper reporters gathering outside the house, waiting for Diego to leave so they could get their story. This was not the nicest thing to have done. It must be quite hard to be famous and having everything you do watched by other people.

Mrs Biggs served the dinner and sat down next to Diego.

'This smells delicious. May I?' asked Diego, referring to tasting the food.

'Such wonderful manners. You could learn a thing or two, Billy,' said a very impressed Mrs Biggs.

Diego rolled the spaghetti around his fork before placing it in his mouth. The tomato sauce ran down the side of his face a little as he began chewing. Mrs Biggs smiled as she reached for a serviette.

'I hope you don't mind,' she said, as she wiped the sauce from the corner of his mouth.

'I am so sorry. Forgive me. Billy's description of your cooking was right. It is delicious. It is like what my mama cooks me when I return home.'

A blushing Mrs Biggs said,

'Thank you. That is a compliment.'

They continued eating their food as Billy sat quietly watching Diego Francesco. He couldn't believe that the best player at Birmingham Wanderers was sitting in his dining room eating the spaghetti and meatballs that his mum had cooked and getting on brilliantly with her. He was already hearing wedding bells. A little bit soon, considering they had only met ten minutes ago, but if you are going to dream, you might as well dream big.

'He's right, Mum. It is delicious, as usual,' said Billy.

'Thank you. It is nice being appreciated. Especially by two very handsome men.'

Mrs Biggs realised what she had said and began to blush a little. Diego looked at her and smiled.

'Well, you know what they say. The way to an Italian man's heart is through his stomach,' Diego said, and giggled.

They all laughed. The evening went extremely well. Diego, Billy and Mrs Biggs chatted together all night.

'Please call me Caroline,' she said to Diego as the evening progressed. 'Mrs Biggs seems so formal.'

Billy got to ask Diego lots of questions about football.

'When do you think you will get your first cap for Italy? When did you know you wanted to be a footballer? Were you always so good, or did you need to practise?'

And the questions went on and on. He had so many he wanted to ask that it was a wonder he gave Diego time to answer them.

Finally, it was time for Diego to leave. He was unaware of what was waiting for him outside.

'Billy, could you go and get Diego's coat?' asked Mrs Biggs.

After Billy had gone out of the room, Diego looked at Mrs Biggs and said quietly,

'Caroline, I have had a lovely time this evening. I can't remember the last time I had a nice home-cooked meal. Can I ask if I could take you out, just the two of us, as a thank-you?'

Mrs Biggs became a little embarrassed.

'Really? Me? I am sure you have lots of people who would be willing to go out with you.'

'But I want to spend time with you.'

'Oh, I would love to. Thank you.'

Billy came back with Diego's coat and felt that he had walked into something that perhaps he shouldn't have, as the room became quite silent all of a sudden and Diego and his mum were suddenly not able to look at each other. It was obvious to Billy he had just missed something important, and now they were both embarrassed at him being there.

'Is everything OK?' he asked.

'Yes. Why wouldn't it be?' replied his mum, as she started clearing the plates from the table.

Billy gave Diego his coat and walked to the door. As Billy opened it, he was blinded by flashes of light from the cameras taking pictures in his direction. He quickly closed it again.

'I don't know how this has happened,' said Billy, 'but there are photographers outside.'

'Somebody must have seen you coming in,' said Mrs Biggs, as she joined them at the door.

'I am sorry. This happens to me all the time. I am always being followed by the paparazzi. Everywhere I go they somehow know I am there, and they turn up,' said a very frustrated Diego.

'What are you going to do?' asked Mrs Biggs.

'I will just go outside and give them what they want. Hopefully, they will leave you alone,' said a desperate Diego.

'You don't have to. What if we have some fun first? I have an idea,' said Billy.

'What do you have in mind?' asked Diego.

Billy ran upstairs and returned momentarily carrying a bag of water balloons. Diego saw what he was holding and understood what he had in mind and nodded.

'Very good,' he said.

'You can't do that,' said Mrs Biggs.

'We can. Let's have some fun,' said a grinning Diego.

Mrs Biggs smiled as the three of them filled up the water balloons. They must have filled about twenty balloons by the time they had finished. All the balloons were filled to capacity and ready to pop.

'Be careful,' said a concerned Mrs Biggs. 'We don't want any to explode in the house.'

They crept out of the back door and into the garden before making their way around the side of the house into the shadows of the front garden, where nobody could see them. They each got themselves a very wet and slippery water balloon and launched them in the direction of the waiting journalists. One fell directly onto the head of a journalist waiting at the front of the pack with his huge camera. The other two balloons hit each other in mid-air and exploded over them all. They all looked at each other.

'What was that?' asked one.

'Is it raining?' asked another.

Then another three balloons were catapulted in their direction, and another three and then another three.

'We are under attack,' cried one journalist.

'This ain't right,' cried another.

'Where are they coming from?' asked another.

'We're the press,' cried another. 'We have the right to be here'.

Billy, Mrs Biggs and Diego continued hiding in the shadows of the garden, laughing at the chaos that was erupting on the street.

'Serves them right,' laughed Diego.

'How many have we got left?' asked Mrs Biggs.

'Mme, eight, I think,' said Billy.

'Right. Let's throw them all,' shouted Diego. 'Here we go.'

They picked up the last eight, and one by one they each threw them in the direction of the journalists, who got wetter and wetter as the balloons exploded all over them.

'I have enjoyed myself a lot tonight. Thank you. I need to go while they are still distracted. I will call you soon.'

At that Diego gave Mrs Biggs a kiss on the cheek before running away, as Billy looked on. Mrs Bigg's face went red from blushing.

'What was that?' asked a disgusted Billy.

'He's Italian. It's how they say goodbye,' replied a very happy Caroline. 'Come on. Let's go back inside before they see us.'

They left the drenched reporters outside their house. Diego got into his car and drove next to the reporters and stopped. He put his window down and shouted out,

'See you later, guys.'

'Quick, get your camera,' shouted one of them.

But it was too late. Diego sped off before they could get any kind of photo of him.

CHAPTER 7

It was another day in 4PR at Chilford Academy and another day with Mr Baxter as the class teacher. The children entered the classroom, looked at Mr Baxter, groaned again, and slumped down onto their chairs.

Have you noticed that when you are bored the time seems to go much more slowly than usual, and when you enjoy doing something the time seems to go more quickly? Well, as you can imagine, with Mr Baxter teaching them, the time was going extraordinarily slow. A second seemed like a minute, a minute seemed like an hour, an hour seemed liked a day, and a day seemed like a week.

As Mr Baxter was talking to the children in his very monotone voice, the children's eyelids became heavier and heavier until eventually one child's eyes closed. Mr Baxter saw Peter Queslett's eyes close along with his head resting on his hands on his desktop, and quietly walked over to him before slamming a dictionary down on his desk. Peter quickly woke up.

'Am I boring you, Mr Queslett?' shouted Mr Baxter.

Peter jumped slightly and looked at Mr Baxter.

'You didn't have to shout right down my ear,' responded Peter. 'I think I've gone deaf.'

'Well, I believe I did have to,' replied Mr Baxter, continuing to shout. 'If you have the audacity to fall asleep in my classroom, then you are going to make me very angry. Do you understand?'

Mr Baxter was still being quite obnoxious to the class, and this only seemed to change when another teacher walked into the room. With all the shouting that Mr Baxter did it was likely that the other teachers would have heard him, but nobody had ever come in. However, this time there was a knock at the door, and of course Mr Baxter became all sweetness and kindness for a moment. Mr Jenkins entered the classroom.

'Mr Baxter, can I quickly speak to the children?'

'Of course,' replied Mr Baxter in his very polite manner.

Turning to the class, Mr Jenkins said,

'This won't take long. It's just to let you know that we won't be having trials for the football team at the moment. Disappointingly, only ten children put their names down. This means that as it is seven-a-side football, every one of those children will be taking part in the football competition. So Malcolm, Billy, Chantal and Liberty, I expect to see the four of you in training after school tomorrow.'

As Mr Jenkins finished, the four named children gave out a big cheer. It was the news Billy had been waiting for. Finally, he would get to show everybody his skills and start to become the legend he had always dreamt of becoming. Mr Jenkins left.

'What did I say about the noise?' said a very annoyed Mr Baxter. 'If I hear that again I am not sure you will be attending any football training sessions tomorrow. Have I made myself clear?'

He looked at them sternly, as he was letting them know that he was still the boss. The children stared back at Mr Baxter, secretly hoping that they would never see him again after today.

Some of the children began to daydream and imagine Mr Baxter in different scenarios, which would require him to leave the school forever. Imelda Jenkins imagined a spot growing on the end of his nose, which got bigger and bigger. It got so big that it was as big as his head and then it popped, with the slimy stuff inside it exploding all over him. Mr Baxter ran out of the room holding his nose, never to be seen again. Imelda let out a quiet giggle.

Peter Queslett imagined Mr Baxter suddenly losing his voice. He began to hold his throat and choked until a bee flew out of his mouth. Then another bee, and then another, until eventually his whole body was surrounded by a colony of bees making the loudest buzzing noise. Mr Baxter began screaming and running away from these exceedingly loud insects. One landed on the end of his nose and he flicked it away.

The unhappy bee flew back and stung him on the top of his eyelid, which swelled to the size of a grape almost immediately. He let out the loudest scream and ran out of the classroom. The bees followed and stung him one by one as he ran away, never to be seen again. Peter trembled from the thought and began scratching the back of his neck.

As they returned to the reality of the classroom, they realised that none of their hoped-for scenarios were going to materialise. Mr Baxter was still there.

Finally, after the most boring couple of hours, the morning bell rang for the first break of the day. Without knowing it, Mr Baxter was helping to make the children appreciate Mrs Mulliner even more. They now all realised just how lucky they had been, having her as their teacher.

'I can't believe how bored I am,' said Malcolm.

'I want to go home,' said Peter.

'This day is never going to end,' said Billy.

They sat on a bench staring into space. Mr Baxter had driven the will to learn – if they had ever had it – out of them, and they didn't have the energy to do anything during the break.

'I never realised life could be so dull,' said Malcolm. 'What are we going to do?'

'I think we need to get Mrs Mulliner back where she belongs, in our classroom,' replied Billy. 'We could go to her house after school and beg her to come back.'

'We can't risk Mr Baxter being our teacher tomorrow,' said Peter.

'We can make her a card and get everyone to sign it,' said Billy. 'That usually brings a smile to a teacher's face. All they want is appreciation.'

Children don't usually appreciate just how hard teachers work to educate them and keep them focused throughout the day. They have lessons to plan, books to mark, resources to prepare and children to take care of. Most teachers make this all seem so effortless, and they deserve the best respect they can get from every child and parent in an otherwise thankless occupation. However, Mr Baxter was not one of those teachers. He was someone who gave teachers a bad name. He treated the children like criminals and had no respect for them from the moment he arrived in their classroom.

The bell rang, far too quickly in their opinion, and they all returned to their classroom.

'Come in quietly, please, and sit down,' said Mr Baxter, 'We have a lot to get through.'

As the morning continued, whenever Mr Baxter wasn't looking, the children secretly passed a card around so each child could write a message in it to Mrs Mulliner. They all wrote nice messages in it, explaining how they missed her and wanted her back at school. On the front of the card they each drew a self-portrait. However, because they were Year 4 children, it was going to be quite hard for Mrs Mulliner to guess who drew some of the pictures, as some of them were drawn with stick arms and legs.

Finally, the day – which seemed like a week – ended, and the three boys walked to Mrs Mulliner's house. Normally children don't know where any of their teachers live, and some children even believe that teachers actually live at school and don't ever venture outside of it. However, Bernard Shaw, a pupil in Year 6, lived on the same street as Mrs Mulliner, and he would brag about how he used to see her and go around to her house for cake and tea.

The reality was very different. When Bernard saw her he was like most children who see their teachers outside of school. He became quite embarrassed and tongue-tied, as he didn't quite know what to say to her.

They approached the house and stopped outside it.

'Go on then, Malcolm,' whispered Billy. 'Knock on the door, then.'

'I'm not knocking on it,' replied Malcolm. 'It was your idea. You knock.'

'Peter?' said a hopeful Billy.

'I don't think so.'

So Billy took a deep breath, slowly lifted his hand, and quietly tapped on the door.

'Oh, well, she is not there. Let's go,' said a slightly frightened Billy.

'She won't hear that,' said Malcolm. 'Knock again.'

This time Billy knocked louder and waited for Mrs Mulliner to answer the door. They heard movement inside and prepared themselves to quickly explain why they were there. They were not quite ready for the surprise that awaited them, because when the door opened it wasn't Mrs Mulliner. It was the dinner lady, Mrs Higgins.

'What are you doing here?' said a shocked Peter.

'I live here. What do you want?' replied Mrs Higgins, in her usual unpleasant manner.

'We were looking for Mrs Mulliner,' answered Billy.

'What do you want her for?' asked an agitated Mrs Higgins.

'Never mind. We have the wrong address,' said Malcolm.

'No, you don't,' said Mrs Higgins, before shouting, 'Nora, it's for you.'

The boys looked at each other and giggled.

'Nora,' laughed Malcolm.

Mrs Mulliner came to the door and looked surprised to see the three boys standing in front of her. They stood there for a moment just staring at their teacher, not knowing what to say. It seemed like a very long time for the boys, but in fact it was only seconds before Malcolm said,

'We miss you.'

Mrs Mulliner smiled.

'We made you this card to ask you to come back to school. We have got the worst teacher in the world taking your place,' said Billy.

'Please come back,' said Peter.

Mrs Mulliner invited the children into her house. Curiosity overwhelmed them, so they went inside. She lived in a small mid-terraced house. The inside was very clean, neat and tidy, with everything in its right place. Mrs Mulliner didn't like mess, but the children already knew this as she always insisted that they tidied the classroom each day before they went home. It felt like a very nice home, and as soon as they sat down the children felt very welcome.

'All the children wrote on your card,' said Billy.

'It took us all day to complete,' continued Peter.

Mrs Mulliner sat for a moment looking at the card. She smiled when she saw the drawings and read the messages. Her eyes began to water, and a tear made its way down her cheek.

'Thank you, boys. This is very sweet.'

'Please come back. I am sure the person who put the frog in your coffee is really sorry,' said Malcolm.

The smile momentarily left her, as she remembered the reason why she had stayed away from school over the last couple of days.

'I am sure they are,' replied Mrs Mulliner. 'Now tell me, what has my replacement been doing during my absence?'

The boys took turns explaining what had been happening over the last couple of days. The words 'mean' and 'shouting' and 'boredom' were used quite a lot during their ten minutes of explanation. Mrs Mulliner had a hurt expression on her face, as if to show her disapproval at what had been going on in her classroom.

Finally, she said,

'I see.'

After a moment of silence, she continued.

'You know, boys, over these last few days I have discovered something new, which I think everybody should know about and do.'

The boys looked at each other. They couldn't say anything at that moment, but they knew what was about to be said. Mrs Mulliner had been reading a new self-help book and she was about to share it with them.

'Yes, here we go,' they thought.

'I have been reading … about the power of forgiveness. I have been learning how forgiveness helps you to let go of the past and allows you to move forward. I have been working on this over the last couple of days.'

The boys looked at each other, unsure how to respond.

'I am thinking of introducing it to the class, perhaps on a Friday, and calling it Forgiveness Friday.'

'Well, it is Friday tomorrow, miss. Does that mean you are coming back?' asked a hopeful Billy.

'After such a nice card, how could I refuse? I can't let you all down, can I?' replied a smiling Mrs Mulliner.

The boys stood up and ran over to her and gave her a big hug.

'Oh, thank you, miss,' said a very happy Billy.

'Miss,' said Malcolm, 'Why is Mrs Higgins here?'

'She is a special friend of mine,' replied Mrs Mulliner, 'and we live together. That's all you need to know... Now off you go. Your parents will be worried.'

CHAPTER 8

Billy arrived home full of relief that he wouldn't have to have Mr Baxter as his teacher any longer. As he walked into the house, he saw his mum looking in the hallway mirror and applying some bright red lipstick. Billy walked over and stared.

'Mum, why are you wearing lipstick?' he asked.

Mrs Biggs continued applying the lipstick. When she had finished, she replied,

'Natalie from next door will be here to babysit you in five minutes. Your dinner is on the table, and I am going out for a couple of hours.'

'But you never go out, and why is Natalie coming? She is only fifteen, and I am old enough to look after myself,' said a stunned Billy.

'Well, I am tonight… Diego called and wants to take me out for dinner, and it is against the law to leave a nine-year-old child on their own, so that is why Natalie is coming,' said a smiling Mrs Biggs, who was now getting very nervous and beginning to feel quite like a teenager again, even though she was thirty-one.

'Twice in one week? Why can't I come? He's my friend too.'

'Perhaps another time, Billy. Tonight is Mummy night.'

The doorbell rang and Billy answered the door. In front of him stood Natalie, wearing an already bored expression, with her back leaning against the wall as if she didn't have enough energy to stand upright. She was wearing her usual headphones and was still in her school uniform. Billy stared at her for a moment while blocking the doorway.

He didn't want her to come inside the house. Natalie had babysat Billy once before but they were not the best of friends, like some children are with their sitters. In fact, the last time Natalie was there she only managed to say two words to him all night, which were,

'Bed, now.'

Natalie wasn't big on conversation. She liked her music, and whenever Billy or Mrs Biggs passed her on the street, she would have her headphones on and grunt as they passed her. That was the evening Billy was going to have to look forward to – an evening of nothingness – while his mum was out with the great Diego.

'Well, are you gonna let me in?' Natalie said, and grunted.

'Six words today,' thought Billy. He didn't reply. He just opened the door wider, and Natalie walked in.

'Hello, Natalie. Nice to see you again,' said Mrs Biggs in a very pleasant way.

'OK,' replied Natalie.

'Well, my mobile number is on the fridge if you need me, but I am sure everything will be fine,' said Mrs Biggs, 'Now, Billy, bed by eight. No later.'

Billy just stared at his mum disapprovingly. Not only had she made him feel like a small child by having a babysitter – *baby* being the operative part of the word – but now in front of Natalie she was telling the whole world what time he went to bed. It was so embarrassing. She gave Billy a kiss and put her coat on.

'Natalie, I will be back around ten,' she said.

'OK,' replied Natalie.

'Well, it was nice talking to you,' said Mrs Biggs. It could have been in a sarcastic manner, but it wasn't. She was too excited to care.

Once Mrs Biggs had left the house Natalie walked into the lounge and closed the door behind her, leaving Billy alone, in silence, in the hallway. He walked into the kitchen and began eating his dinner of chicken, peas and chips.

'Bribery food,' he thought. But he didn't care. Yummy.

A little while later the doorbell rang. Billy ran to the door, thinking his mum must be home a little earlier than planned. However, if he had stopped to think about it, he would have realised it wouldn't be his mum, as she had a key. And it was far too early, even if things hadn't gone too well between her and Diego.

Just as he was about to open the door, he heard Natalie's voice from behind him.

'Stop,' she said, sounding very unfriendly. Billy turned around and saw somebody that looked a little like Natalie, but he couldn't be sure that it was her. The person standing in front of him had had a complete transformation. Her hair was combed and hung neatly to her shoulders, and she was wearing make-up and a rainbow sequins dress. The most bewildering thing for Billy was that she wasn't wearing her usual headwear of a set of headphones.

'Who are you?' he asked. 'And what have you done with Natalie?'

'Move away from the door – it's for me – and off you go. Go and read your comics or go and play one of your games. Just don't let me hear from you for the rest of the night.'

Billy didn't move. The doorbell rang again. Natalie stared at Billy until it became uncomfortable, so he decided to do what she asked and went upstairs. However, instead of going to his bedroom, he decided to wait at the top of the stairs to see who it was.

Natalie opened the door and standing in front of her was a boy of about sixteen, wearing jeans and a leather jacket.

'All right, babe?' he said.

Natalie didn't answer. She just jumped on him, wrapped her legs around his waist and began to kiss him. Billy pulled a disgusted face. After witnessing this show of affection, he felt as if he were going to vomit. Although Natalie was simply giving the boy a kiss, it was all a bit too much for Billy. But he continued watching them as Natalie led the boy into the lounge. Then he suddenly heard Natalie shouting,

'Bedroom, now,' so he raced into his room. He couldn't believe this was how his day was ending, with him stuck in his bedroom, and after doing such a nice thing as getting Mrs Mulliner to return to school as well.

He threw himself on his bed and looked at his football posters. A thumping noise, which might be classed as music by some people, could be heard coming from the lounge, along with Natalie giggling. Billy couldn't remember ever seeing her smile, and he had lived next door to her all his life. What was the world coming to.

However, the world hadn't changed that much, as suddenly the music stopped, the giggling turned to shouting and Billy heard the front door opening before slamming shut. Then the lounge door slammed shut. Billy waited for a moment. Silence had returned to the house. He walked down to the lounge door and listened outside. Nothing but silence. He slowly opened the door and looked inside. Natalie was lying on the sofa with her headphones on, listening to music.

'Are you OK?' he asked.

'Get out,' shouted Natalie.

Billy was going to be a sympathetic friend to Natalie, listening to her problems, but instead realised that their relationship was probably never going to change, so he returned to his bedroom. He lay on his bed and slowly drifted off into dreamland.

CHAPTER 9

Finally, the day of the first football match had arrived. There was a feeling of excitement around the team, as none of the players had played for the school team before. In fact, most of them had never played for any team before. Even though Billy dreamt of being a footballer and pictured achieving his goal, this was the first game he would ever have played.

For Billy this was the most important day of his life. This was his chance to shine, and to show everybody just how good he was. It was his chance to show Mr Jenkins that he was wrong to stop him playing football every day at school, and that it was hindering his ability. He imagined football scouts watching the game and arguing over who would sign him.

However, the reality was quite different, and it was a complete shock for Billy and his teammates. This was because Billy's dreams didn't quite match his ability. Yes, he was constantly talking about football and yes, he was always kicking a football around his garden, but his real-life ability was not in the same league as the skills that he saw himself having in his mind, so when the game had finished Billy was quite disappointed with what had actually occurred. There were far more lowlights than highlights in the game.

On far too many occasions, when Billy had the ball, he would try to dribble it down the field, but would often trip over for no apparent reason and land on his bottom, and then the player in the opposing team would simply take the ball away from him. On other occasions, when Billy needed to control the ball, instead of stopping the ball it would simply roll under his foot and go towards the other team. On those rare occasions when he didn't fall over and did manage to control the ball, he would try to cross the ball to a teammate. However, the ball would hardly lift off the floor and would trickle to a player in the opposing team instead.

It seemed that every time he had the ball, the opposite team would simply have to wait for Billy to lose it of his own accord and they would retrieve it without having to make any effort at all. It would be gifted to them.

Perhaps the biggest thing that happened in the game was when Malcolm crossed the ball high over the last defender's head and into the box. Then it was just Billy and the goalkeeper. If Billy hit the ball correctly he would score, and they would win the game.

However, when the ball went over the player's head and dropped, ready to be hit, it bounced. Billy went to kick it but he missed and fell over onto his bottom again, and the ball trickled out for a throw-in.

Luckily, the other team were not much better, and so the game ended 0–0, but Billy's team was not happy with him. They had expected more, considering how much he had made everyone believe he was the next superstar.

On the sidelines, Mr Jenkins couldn't believe what he was seeing. They were so close to winning the game, but Billy had missed, and they hadn't. He was jumping up and down in frustration, and rubbing his eyes in disbelief with his fingers. It wasn't a pretty sight, either, because Mr Jenkins had a large tummy. As he jumped up his tummy went down, and as he came down his tummy went up. On some occasions it looked like his tummy might actually hit him in his face, it was moving around so much. But fortunately it didn't.

Anyway, Mr Jenkins wasn't very happy with what he had seen, and Billy's teammates let him know they weren't either.

'I thought you were meant to be good,' said a frustrated and tired Jack as he walked past Billy and brushed into him with his shoulder, and not in a nice way.

'I think you would be better off as a bus driver, the amount of time you spent on your bottom … you loser,' said an angry Ismail.

'Or a swimmer, the number of times you dived… Get it? Swimmer, diving…' said an amused Liberty.

Billy's face fell as he walked over to collect his belongings. Malcolm walked over to him and put his arm around his shoulder.

'They think I'm rubbish,' said a crestfallen Billy.

'Don't worry about it,' replied Malcolm supportively. 'Nobody was really outstanding today. We were all rubbish.'

'I don't know what happened. I thought I was better than that.'

'It's only a game. It's not the end of the world,' said Malcolm, trying to make his best friend feel better.

But he wasn't able to. Everything Billy had ever thought and did had led him to that moment. Unfortunately, what he thought was going to happen didn't happen. In his mind, he was going to get the ball, run around all the players in the opposing team and score a hat-trick. The reality was quite different. Everybody thought he was a loser, a joke.

When he got home, his mum was waiting for him.

'Well, how did you get on?' she asked.

'We drew 0–0,' Billy replied.

'That's not too bad, for your first game.'

'I suppose,' responded Billy.

'Go and wash your hands. Dinner is nearly ready.'

Billy took his bag to his bedroom, threw it on the bed and looked at all his football posters. He looked at each poster as a tear trickled down his cheek. Billy's dreams were beginning to fade away because of the first game that he had ever played. He wanted to curl up in his bed and hide away from the world. He had failed, and he wanted to give up. He grabbed the corner of his Roberto Di Luga poster and was about to rip it off the wall when Di Luga shouted,

'No. Nobody is perfect the first time they do something. I am a professional footballer now, but I practised and practised when I was younger. If I couldn't do something I practised some more. That is why I am the best defender now.'

'What if I am not good enough?' asked Billy.

'Never say that. You have confidence. Never let anybody take that confidence away from you. Confidence is ninety per cent of achieving anything.'

Luckily, Billy really loved football, so he didn't rip the poster off his wall.

What he was beginning to realise was that when something in your life doesn't quite go to plan you have to analyse what went wrong, dust yourself down, and try again. The most successful people in the world make lots of mistakes and fail constantly. People only see their successes.

Even Diego Francesco and José Fernandes needed to practise and practise, and they had both had their moments when things didn't quite go to plan. But winners don't quit. They learn from their failures, move on, don't make the same mistakes again, and make sure that it all makes them a better person.

That is exactly what Billy did. This time he was going to take the advice of the players on his posters, and so after dinner he went into his garden and began to practise. What he practised that evening was ball control. He wanted to make sure that whenever a ball came to him in the future, he would be able to stop it and control it. Billy practised and practised until his legs hurt and he struggled to keep his eyes open from tiredness. He enjoyed himself and knew that he was already improving.

Little did he know that somebody was going to enter his life and help change it forever.

CHAPTER 10

Billy had been practising in his garden after school every day since the first football match. He had been watching videos on the Internet of footballers training, so that he could copy what they were doing.

Since today was a weekend day he decided to go to the park, as there was more space there to train. He had been practising the different training techniques when he noticed a man kicking a ball around all on his own. Billy stopped what he was doing and watched the almost magical techniques that the man had developed and was mesmerised by what he saw. A technique that particularly caught Billy's attention was when the man kicked the ball high up into the air, jumped up, did a 360-degree turn, and as the ball dropped, kicked it into the top corner of the goal, all without touching the floor.

Billy began to clap but realised where he was, and so stopped before looking around to check that nobody had seen him. He continued watching as the man repeated the movement, as if to show that it was not a chance occurrence. Billy rubbed his eyes to check that what he was watching was actually happening, and not a figment of his imagination. Surely what was happening was impossible, yet there the man was, doing it.

Next the man flicked the ball high over his head and did an overhead kick, straight into the top left-hand corner of the net, before again repeating it for good measure. Billy could not take his eyes off the man. He had never seen anything like it before. Not even professionals did these kinds of tricks in the Premier League.

Billy moved closer to the man and began to watch him intently. He watched what he was doing and then tried to copy him, but the tricks the man was doing were quite difficult and Billy found them quite impossible to copy.

Billy decided that he had to speak to him to find out who he was and how he had developed such a magnificent technique. But he knew that you should never talk to strangers unless you are with an adult and are given permission to do so. Billy's mum had told him many times about the dangers of talking to strangers in the street. Normally Billy did what he was told, but in that moment he forgot everything he had been taught and was drawn to the man. It was almost as if a rope had been tied around his waist and he was being slowly pulled towards him.

'Are you a professional footballer?' asked Billy.

The man stopped for a moment and looked at Billy curiously. From a distance, from the way the man had been moving and playing, Billy had assumed that he must have been no older than twenty, but close up Billy could see that in fact he was a lot older, and possibly in his fifties or even his sixties. He was an athletic sixty, though, and like an incredible grandfather who was able to play football even better than the professionals.

Billy hadn't noticed it before, but as the man looked at him he saw that there was a kind of glow surrounding him, almost like an aura. This made the man seem even more magical. Billy stared at him for a moment, transfixed, before the man finally answered him with a simple,

'No.'

'Wow. You are amazing. How did you get so good?' asked Billy.

Billy thought that what he had seen was better than anything he had ever seen from any footballer that had ever lived. He couldn't understand how such an outstanding talent had never played football professionally. It made him think that perhaps he wasn't good enough after all. If this man had never been discovered, with his talent, then how would he be? But then he remembered what Roberto Di Luga had said about confidence and immediately dismissed it from his mind.

'A lot of effort and dedication,' replied the man.

'Do you think you could teach me?' asked Billy.

The man looked Billy up and down.

'I'm not sure. Does your mother know that you talk to strangers with no thought for your safety?'

Billy took a step back away from the man. The man was right. He did not know him and he really shouldn't be talking to strangers, but he couldn't help himself. There was something about him. Something that made him realise that this man could be trusted. Billy felt safe but asked anyway,

'You're not dangerous, are you?'

'No, but wouldn't a dangerous man say that too?'

'Please teach me,' begged Billy.
The man threw Billy a ball.

'Let me see what you can do.'

Billy ran around, showing him the various techniques that he had been learning over the last few days. He dribbled, flicked the ball up in the air, and ran, changing direction as he went. After he had finished he gave the ball back to the man.

The man began to walk away. Billy stopped and stared, thinking that he was about to stop and kick the ball to him from a distance, but he did not stop and continued to walk away. Then suddenly he said,

'Be here straight after school on Tuesday, and don't be late.'

'I won't,' replied a very pleased Billy.

Billy picked up his ball and was about to ask the man a question, but when he looked back in his direction he was nowhere to be seen. Billy looked around to see where he possibly could have gotten to, but he was gone. He couldn't believe what he had seen and how lucky he was to have such a talent to train him. He knew that Tuesday was going to be the start of something great.

What Billy didn't know, and would never discover, was that the man had been there for a reason. He had been expecting Billy to be at the park on that day and at that precise moment in time. He knew Billy would ask him to train him, and he knew he would train Billy and how to get the best out of him. This was where Billy's daydreaming techniques began to become a reality.

CHAPTER 11

As it was Monday morning, the children in 4PR were busy imagining their futures. Sally O'Malley arrived in class late but rather than disturb them, she waited at the side of the room until they had finished their session. This was the first time Sally had been back at school since the incident with the laxatives.

When the alarm on Mrs Mulliner's phone rang for the session to end, everybody opened their eyes and immediately laid them on Sally. She looked around the room at all the eyes staring back at her, then looked at Mrs Mulliner. She slowly and shyly walked over to her table and stopped. She looked Mrs Mulliner in the eyes and said,

'I am sorry for being late.'

'That's OK. It's good to have you back,' replied Mrs Mulliner.

Sally continued to stand in front of her. Everyone continued looking, intrigued by what was happening.

'Is there anything else?'

Sally opened her mouth and whispered,

'It was me.'

'Sorry, Sally. I couldn't quite catch that.'

'It was me who put the frog in your coffee.'

'Oh, I see,' replied Mrs Mulliner with a sad and disappointed expression on her face.

'I want to say sorry.'

'Well, go on, then,' said Mrs Mulliner.

'I'm sorry, and it won't happen again.'

'I should think not. Now go and sit down.'

Sally picked up her bag and quickly walked to her desk and sat down without looking at any of the other children. Silence continued to hang over the room, as the children's eyes followed her to her desk. They couldn't believe that Mrs Mulliner had been so forgiving and had not given Sally any form of punishment. She had been practising her forgiveness techniques, and they were obviously helping her. Mrs Mulliner looked at the class and said,

'It took a lot of courage to do what Sally just did, and I am very grateful that she did it. Let this be a lesson about apologising for your mistakes and about forgiveness.'

After what Mrs Mulliner had said to the class, all Billy and Malcolm could think about during the morning lessons was what they had done to Sally and whether they should apologise to her. After all, was what they did to her really a fitting punishment for Sally cheating or had they gone a little overboard? A feeling of guilt began to hang over them. At dinner time, by the time they had reached the dinner hall, they were convinced that they needed to apologise.

'Well?' asked Mrs Higgins in her usual manner.

'Good afternoon, Mrs Higgins, and what a lovely day,' said Malcolm with a smile.

'What are you after?' replied Mrs Higgins.

'What lovely nourishment do we have today?' asked Billy.

Mrs Higgins looked at them with a confused expression on her face. She was holding a very large serving spoon in her hand while waiting to serve them.

'Well, you can have this,' she said, pointing to the food. 'Or this,' she added, pointing to the spoon, 'and you know where I could put it, don't ya?'

Billy gulped.

'I think I will have the food, thank you.'

Mrs Higgins poured the green goo that was meant to be food onto Billy and Malcolm's trays, and then they walked to the nearest available table. Malcolm got a spoonful of the green goo, also known as lunch. He dipped the tip of his tongue into it and grimaced.

'Disgusting,' he said. 'This must surely be classed as child abuse.'

He then pushed the tray to the side of the table, opened his bag and pulled out a king-size Mars bar. Billy gave it a look of longing.

'You don't have another one, do you?' asked Billy.

'As a matter of fact I do. Ta-dah.'

Malcolm pulled out another Mars bar and gave it to Billy.

'You're such a good friend,' said Billy.

As they began to eat their chocolate bars, Sally nervously walked into the cafeteria alone, trying not to be noticed, and unsure what reaction she would receive from the rest of the school. The other children stopped momentarily and looked at her, but then continued with what they were doing. Billy and Malcolm looked over at her. She walked to the food counter and politely asked for some food. Mrs Higgins threw a dollop of the green goo onto her plate.

'Can I have some more, please?' she asked.

Mrs Higgins looked at Sally in disbelief, as she had never been asked that before. She poured more food onto her tray. Sally then walked to the table that Billy and Malcolm were sitting at.

'Is it OK if I sit here?' whispered Sally.

They both nodded and Sally sat down. She sniffed the food and grimaced. Billy and Malcolm kept staring at each other and nodding in the direction of Sally. After a few moments of silence Billy decided to be brave and said,

'Sally, I want to—'

'Hmm,' interrupted Malcolm.

'Sorry, we want to apologise to you. We were the ones who caused you to have that accident in assembly—'

'We put laxatives in your scone,' interrupted Malcolm. 'We didn't mean for it to get so out of hand. It is just that—'

'We discovered you cheated and filled the competition box up with your name,' continued Billy.

Sally stood and picked up her tray. She was unusually tall for her age and was head and shoulders above anybody in her class.

If you look in the mirror, you will see that you have two eyebrows. But Sally didn't. Her left eyebrow started on the left-hand side of her face and joined in the middle with her right eyebrow to form one long eyebrow. She also looked like she had three eyes, as she had a mole in the centre of her forehead just above her single eyebrow.

When she was younger Sally had to listen to lots of teasing from the other children. This was not very nice, and it made Sally the kind of girl that she was now: a mean girl. When she had her unusually rapid growth spurt she learnt to take care of herself, and took revenge on the children who had bullied her. The irony was that she then became like them herself: a bully.

After picking up her tray, Sally poured her food all over Billy's head without saying a word. The other children in the cafeteria stopped and looked in their direction. A stunned silence filled the room as the green goo slowly dripped down Billy's face.

Sally then picked up Billy and Malcolm's trays and poured more green goo over Malcolm's head. Finally, she got a large jug of water and poured half of it inside Malcolm's trousers, and the other half inside Billy's.

'I am not stupid. I had time to think while I was off, and the conclusion I came to was that it had to be the scone that caused my accident. I also knew that you wouldn't admit to it unless I made you feel guilty. My apology to Mrs Mulliner was not real. It was just an act to get you two fools to own up.'

She took the Mars bar from Malcolm's hand, took a bite, and stormed towards the door of the cafeteria. At the exit she stopped, turned around and shouted,

'Losers.'

She left the cafeteria and heard a loud cheer from all the other children in the cafeteria. Her lips momentarily curled as she allowed herself a very quick and satisfied smile.

Billy and Malcolm sat quietly for a moment before standing up and wiping the food off their faces. The other children began shouting,

'Loser, loser, loser.' A Year 6 child used the situation to throw his food at them, which in turn caused a food fight to break out. Food was thrown this way and that way all over the cafeteria.

During the fight you would probably expect a sensible adult to call the headmaster or the nearest teacher, but Mrs Higgins was not a sensible adult. She picked up her largest spoon and filled it with the green goo, and when a child walked past, she aimed it and threw it like a missile in their direction.

Splat. Straight over the back of their head. She then looked away, as if she had no idea what was happening. That is until another child happened to cross her path, and another missile happened to land on them.

When Mr Hussain finally arrived in the cafeteria, Mrs Higgins slowly and quietly moved away from the area and hid behind the huge cooker, so she would not be seen as a perpetrator.

'Stop,' shouted Mr Hussain.

Mrs Higgins came back out from behind the cooker and gave a performance worthy of an Oscar.

'Oh, Mr Hussain, I am so glad you have arrived. It was like carnage in here. The children are running riot. I tried to stop them, but they wouldn't listen.'

'That's OK, Mrs Higgins. It is not your fault.' He turned to the children. 'I want to see every single one of you cleaning up this mess now. A letter will be going out to all your parents about your behaviour tonight. Now get started.'

The children quietly and reluctantly began cleaning the cafeteria.

'You are so commanding,' said Mrs Higgins to Mr Hussain.

Mr Hussain quickly walked away without saying a word.

CHAPTER 12

At the end of the school day, the football team got together for their next match. They were all changed and waiting in the changing room for Mr Jenkins to arrive and announce the team. Billy had been looking forward to this match. After all, he had been practising every day and wanted to show his teammates and Mr Jenkins how much he had improved.

Unfortunately, Mr Jenkins was not in a very forgiving mood. Because of the mistakes Billy had made in the last game, he had decided to drop Billy to the substitutes bench. Billy could not believe what had happened. He sat on the bench momentarily, staring into space, unable to move, as the reality of not starting the game sank in.

Even after everything he had done to try and make amends for the last game, he was now on the bench... Billy Biggs, future football superstar, unable to help his team achieve their goal of winning the trophy at Valley Park.

It felt like the end of the world to him. Mr Jenkins had taken everything away from him in that one moment.

Billy returned to Planet Earth as the shock began to slowly pass. He decided he would not let it affect him, and he was going to make sure that he was prepared for when Mr Jenkins needed him to play. So Billy did his warm-up by running up and down the side of the pitch. He stretched his legs, he stretched his arms, and then he repeated it all over again, all time looking at Mr Jenkins, in the hope he would call him over and put him on the pitch. When he did not do this, he made sure that Mr Jenkins couldn't forget he was there as he stood next to him, and occasionally asked,

'When can I go on, sir?'

'When I'm fit and ready,' Mr Jenkins would reply.

Unfortunately, Mr Jenkins was not very fit and so he was never ready. He didn't give Billy the opportunity to play in that game and he did not let him play in any of the next games either. The team won these games and were doing very well in the league, so Mr Jenkins decided that he needed to keep the team the same. For a boy who lived and breathed football like Billy, he was beyond devastated. After each game he would go home and sit on his bed and talk to his posters, looking for advice.

'You just need to have patience,' said José Fernandes kindly.

'You will get your opportunity. This happens to everybody. It is how you deal with it that shows your true character,' Roberto Di Luga reassured him.

Billy lay there and listened to the advice and tried to stay positive.

Luckily, he still had his Tuesday afternoon coaching sessions. He was enjoying the training and was learning a lot. However, he still hadn't learnt the name of the man. He never thought to ask during the first couple of sessions due to his excitement, and then he felt too embarrassed to ask after that. So, Billy decided to just refer to him as 'Coach'. He felt it showed him respect because he was teaching him all the skills he needed for the future, and it felt appropriate.

Coach seemed happy with the name Billy used for him. But he got Billy's name wrong and called him 'Buddy'. At first Billy thought that it was a term of affection and that it meant 'Friend', but he soon realised that he was mistaken. Coach really thought that it was his name. After weeks of confusion, Billy decided that it would be impolite to correct him and so he continued to answer to that name.

During these training sessions with Coach, Billy felt like anything was possible. When he made mistakes, Coach showed him what he was doing wrong and corrected him. What really pleased Billy was how quickly he was learning and improving. Each week Coach would give more and more praise, and fewer and fewer instructions.

Finally, during the last session, before the most important game of the season, Coach told Billy,

'You are ready.'

Billy looked at Coach and gave him a huge hug. He appreciated everything he had done for him, and after hugging for a moment he realised he couldn't let go of him.

'Please come to the game if we get to the final at Valley Park. I want you to help me if I make a mistake.' Then he thought, 'If Mr Jenkins lets me play, of course.'

'You will get your chance. I can foresee it… Is this what you want?'

'Yes,' replied Billy.

'Then I will be there... Now you must go home. It is getting late.'

Billy squeezed him one last time before finally letting go. What Billy had suddenly realised, even though he had spent many weeks training with him, was that not only did he not know his name, but he also knew very little about him. He was in his fifties or sixties, with a full head of silver hair, and always dressed in the same pure white tracksuit, but whenever Billy tried to have a conversation with him, he would tell Billy to concentrate and continue with his training. At the end of each session he would leave, and it would seem like he just vanished, just like the first time they met. Billy had no idea where he lived or where he went.

Today, however, Billy was determined to find out where he went after each session. After all, if Coach decided not to turn up at Valley Park, or, even worse, if they didn't get to the final, Billy wouldn't know where to find him. So, when Coach started to walk away, Billy didn't take his eyes off him and began to follow him. He made sure that there was very little distance between him and Coach, just enough so that he wouldn't be seen.

However, Billy's plan didn't work. When Coach walked behind the only large bush in the park and went momentarily out of sight, Billy ran to catch him up. But it was too late. He was gone.

'How is that possible?' Billy said out loud. 'What's going on?'

It was impossible, just like the football tricks that Coach had been doing on the day they had met. Impossible was definitely the correct word to use, since there was nothing else in sight to hide behind. There were no trees, no fences, no more bushes even. Just a clear view to the end of the park.

Billy ran around the bush, just to make certain that Coach wasn't playing a trick on him, but there was no Coach. Just like magic, he was gone.

Billy stood silently for a moment, to assess the situation. He thought of three reasons how this could have possibly happened.

First, Coach was a magician, and he could use his clever illusions to hide. This could be possible, because magicians are very good at hiding things until the moment they choose to reveal them.

Second, Coach was part of Billy's imagination. Billy did have a great imagination, but how would Billy improve if Coach existed only in his mind? Most of the things he had taught Billy couldn't be found on the Internet. He knew this was the case because he had tried searching and people might have found him strange if they had seen him talking to himself in the park.

Third, he was Billy's guardian angel, who had been sent to make him the best footballer in the world.

Billy just smiled, shook his head in disbelief, and dismissed the thoughts before walking home. He was getting hungry. Running around after a football is enough to make anybody peckish.

Billy preferred option three.

CHAPTER 13

When Billy arrived home, Diego Francesco was there waiting to have dinner with them. Since the night of the meatballs, Mrs Biggs and Diego had spent a lot of time together. Billy really liked Diego, but he couldn't help feeling just a little bit jealous. After all, it had been only him and his mother his whole life.

'I hope you don't mind, but your mother invited me around for dinner tonight,' said Diego.

Billy looked at him. On the one hand he could have let his jealousy boil over and tell him to get out of the house, that it was his mum, and that Diego didn't belong there. But he looked at his mother and saw just how happy she had become since meeting Diego. She was singing while cooking. She hadn't done that for a very long time. He decided that he couldn't be selfish, and smiled. If his mother had to meet somebody new, then who better than Diego Francesco?

'It's fine,' he said. 'As long as you have a five-minute kickaround with me.'

Diego laughed.

'Just five minutes.'

Billy had been wanting to show somebody the skills he had been developing, and if he couldn't show his teammates on the pitch at least he could show Diego. He began by showing him the trick that had made him approach Coach on that first day. He kicked the ball high up into the air, did a 360-degree turn, and kicked the ball into the net. Diego put his hands on his waist, his jaw dropped open as wide as it could, and he shook his head in disbelief.

'Did I really just see that with my own eyes?' asked Diego.

'You haven't seen anything yet,' giggled Billy.

Billy continued with his football tricks. He ran with the ball then stopped. He put his right foot over the top of it, flicked it up with his left foot, and did a bicycle kick.

'Goal,' shouted Billy. This continued for the full five minutes. It didn't quite turn out to be a kickaround, as Diego never managed to get a kick of the ball. It became the Billy show, as he showed Diego trick after trick.

'I'm stunned,' said Diego. 'What has your mama been feeding you? And give me some.'

'I've just been practising,' smiled Billy.

Diego tried one of the tricks Billy had shown him. He kicked the ball up in the air and did a 360-degree turn. But by the time he went to kick the ball it had already landed on the floor, so Diego ended up kicking thin air and fell, landing on his bottom and knocking his knee with his nose.

'Ouch,' he cried.

'Maybe one day I will show you how to do it,' Billy said, and giggled.

'I hope you get to display that talent at Valley Park,' said an embarrassed Diego.

Billy sighed. Playing at Valley Park had been his dream. He had to play the next game and help the team get to the final. Most of all, he had to be given the opportunity to show everybody what he was capable of.

He knew that his ambition was not just a dream any longer. He had the talent to go with it. It had to happen. He would picture himself playing after dinner. This was going to be the most important imagining he had ever had. He needed to play tomorrow. All his dreams had come to fruition. There was no doubt in his mind that this was going to work too. He went back inside and sat down and had his dinner.

'So, tomorrow is the big day. If you win tomorrow you will get to go to Valley Park,' said his proud mother.

'You will love it,' continued Diego. 'It is such an amazing stadium to play at, and the atmosphere ... *magnifico*. I have never experienced anything like it.'

Billy finished his dinner and went straight to his bedroom, leaving Mrs Biggs and Diego laughing and joking. He lay on his bed and used Mrs Mulliner's technique to get into a meditative state.

He imagined himself playing football the next day. He saw himself get the ball and dribble past three, then four players, before shooting and scoring a goal. He saw all his teammates run over to him and jump on him in celebration after scoring the winning goal and helping his team get to the final. He continued to see this over and over again, until he fell asleep and continued dreaming about the football match.

Mr Jenkins, however, obviously hadn't been tuned in to what Billy had been dreaming about. When the team was announced Billy was again a substitute, as Mr Jenkins had kept the same team as in the previous games. Billy decided to stay positive and to focus on being ready if he was needed.

Today's game was different though, as both teams had the same number of points before the game started and they were both very evenly matched.

At half-time the game was 0–0. Then, as the second half began, within five minutes Chilford Academy gave away a penalty. The player who stepped forward to take it was called Hugo. But really he should have been named Humungous, as he towered over everybody in both teams – so much so that he looked thirteen, not nine.

He placed the ball on the spot, looked up, and stared at the goalkeeper for a whole minute before taking the penalty. Chantal, the goalkeeper, tried to stare back, but she couldn't hold eye contact for very long and looked away. And at that precise moment the penalty was taken, and Hugo scored. So now it was 1–0.

With ten minutes to go, the game was still at 1–0 when Hugo went crashing into Liberty, pushing her over with his shoulder and stepping on her ankle. She was in pain and rolled around on the grass. Mr Jenkins ran on to the pitch and saw that she had a large cut and bruise on her ankle and could not continue playing any longer. He helped her on to her good foot, and she hobbled off the pitch.

Billy looked at Mr Jenkins. Mr Jenkins looked at Billy. Mr Jenkins looked at Scott, the other substitute, and then looked back at Billy. With a despondent look he said,

'On you go, Billy.'

To say that Billy ran onto the pitch would be the wrong description, as he was more floating than running. This was the moment he had been waiting for. All those games where he had to watch rather than play had come down to this moment. They had to score to get to the final, not just one goal but two.

With nine minutes to go Billy got his first touch of the ball. He tried to dribble past one player but got tackled and heard a big groan from the other players.

'Here we go again,' shouted one. With seven minutes to go, Billy again got the ball. He looked up and saw his teammates surrounding him.

'Pass,' shouted one, and,

'Pass,' shouted another.'

'Go, Billy, you can do it,' shouted Malcolm. Billy hit the ball in front of him and ran on to catch up with it. He went around one player, he went around two players, he went around three players. He looked up, saw the goalkeeper off his line, hit it high over his head... It was going ... going ... going... It was gone, as it hit the top of the post and went out for a goal kick.

With five minutes to go, Malcolm had the ball down the left wing. He looked up and Billy ran into the box. Malcolm crossed the ball but it looked like it was going behind Billy. But instead of leaving it he jumped, did a bicycle kick, hit the ball and watched it travel into the top right-hand corner of the net,

'Goal...', everyone shouted, as one.

The score was now 1–1.

All the players ran over to Billy and jumped on him as a wall of bodies lined up on top of each other and created a tower. It was a wonder Billy could breathe with so many children on top of him.

Mr Jenkins jumped up and down, cheering. What he didn't realise was that Liberty was sitting in front of him, hidden by his tummy, so when he jumped up his stomach hit her on the head, and when he came down his stomach hit her on the head again. This continued until she lay on the ground to get out of his way. She wiped off the sweat from her forehead that had been transferred from his stomach. Yuck.

The players all got up, and Billy gasped for air once he was able to breathe properly again. There were now only three minutes left, but at least they had managed to bring the game level again. They were beginning to think about penalties and who might take them.

Hugo, on the other hand, had a different plan in mind. He was going to wait until Billy had the ball and do the hardest sliding tackle he had ever done, and was going to make sure that he got the ball but also got Billy's leg at the same time. He wasn't a very nice boy, as you have probably already guessed, and he definitely looked closer to thirteen than he did nine.

With one minute to go Billy got the ball. He dribbled past two players and he could clearly see that Hugo was running directly towards him. In Billy's mind he seemed to be howling like a wolf, but no doubt he was just out of breath.

Billy ran towards the goal and was about to score when Hugo slid, with his studs facing Billy's ankle. He hit Billy's ankle and the ball. Billy fell to the ground and yelled in pain. The referee ran over to check on him. Mr Jenkins bounced onto the pitch to see if he was OK.

Billy lay on the floor clutching his ankle, but he was determined to finish the game and not let this opportunity come to an end. He stood up and hobbled towards the ball. He placed it on the spot where the tackle occurred and lined up to take the free kick.

'Are you sure you're OK to continue, Billy?' asked a very concerned Mr Jenkins.

Billy nodded and looked towards the goal. The referee looked at Hugo and showed him the red card. Hugo looked at him in disbelief. He started arguing with the referee.

'You can't do that. I got the ball.'

'You got half his leg as well,' replied the referee. 'Now get off my pitch.'

Hugo walked over to Billy and stood in front of him. Billy could only see his chest, so he had to look up to see his face. Hugo looked down at him and said,

'You will miss.'

Billy smiled and replied,

'We'll see.'

Billy noticed a few hairs growing above Hugo's top lip. He stopped and stared at them. Then suddenly, he felt an urge that he couldn't stop. His hand slowly began to rise and move in the direction of Hugo's lip, and he pulled one of his hairs out. Hugo screamed in pain and grabbed the top of his lip. Hugo stopped and looked at Billy, but the referee stepped between them both.

The referee looked at Hugo and pointed towards the side of the pitch.

'Leave the pitch. Now,' he insisted.

Hugo slowly walked off the pitch, so that Billy would have to wait even longer before taking the free kick. The referee looked at Billy and smiled. Billy took three steps back and looked in the direction of the goal. He took a deep breath, ran towards the ball, and kicked it high in the direction of the goal. Normally this would all happen very quickly, but since this was an important moment of the game, for everybody watching and playing, it seemed to happen in slow motion, just like you see in the movies.

The ball hit the side of the post as the goalkeeper dived to save it. The ball came out from the goal and hit the goalkeeper on the back of his head, before slowly trickling into the net.

'Goal…'

From the sidelines Hugo could see what had happened. His teacher looked at him and said,

'I can't believe you let a Year 4 boy embarrass you like that. You're four years older than all of them out there.'

So he was thirteen after all.

On the pitch the Chilford Academy team were cheering and singing as the final whistle was blown. The team had made it to the finals.

'We're off to Valley Park, we're off to Valley Park… And now you'd better believe us, and now you'd better believe us, and now you'd better believe us… We're off to Valley Park,' chanted the whole team.

Billy had finally got his chance and had proven to the team, but most importantly to himself, that he had the skills to become a great footballer. The players picked him up and lifted him above their heads. Well, Mr Jenkins picked him up. The children helped a little.

This was his best day ever.

CHAPTER 14

The next day the team arrived back at school and were welcomed like heroes. During yet another assembly Mr Hussain stood proudly on the stage.

'Yesterday, the under tens football team got through to the final of the Birmingham Wanderers Shield, winning 2–1. I want to take this opportunity to let them know how proud we are of them and show our appreciation for their hard work and determination... If I could ask the team to come up onto the stage, please.'

The players looked at each other, embarrassed and a little unsure about whether they wanted to go up in front of the whole school. Billy was the first one to stand up, and this led the others to follow him. They eventually all stood on the stage, looking proud but a little self-conscious at what they had achieved. They had to wait a moment as Liberty slowly limped her way onto the stage.

'I am sure we all wish them the very best when they play at Valley Park next Saturday against Stafford Primary School. They will then be able to stay and watch the Birmingham Wanderers vs Manchester United game from the VIP seats.'

The players all looked at each other and smiled at the surprise announcement.

'Good luck, and let's give them a huge clap.'

The children clapped as the players left the stage and returned to their places. They all felt ten feet tall, as this was the proudest moment of their lives, although this would undoubtedly change once they had played on the pitch at Valley Park.

The Saturday of the game couldn't come quickly enough for Billy. He had marked it down on his calendar with a drawing of a football, and crossed each day off as it passed, getting one step closer with each cross.

Finally, it was the night before the game. Billy couldn't sleep, as he was too excited. He knew that there wouldn't be many fans in the stadium to watch them play, as fans tended to arrive closer to the actual kick-off time of the main game. However, this didn't matter to him. What mattered was the excitement of playing on the same pitch that many of his heroes had graced before him.

Billy finally got out of bed at 6 a.m. and quietly walked downstairs, so as not to wake his mum. He got out his football boots and polished them until they were sparklingly clean. He then got out his shin pads and football kit and placed them in his bag along with his boots.

He was ready. He was ready to show the world that he deserved to be signed by the Birmingham Wanderers academy. It would be the start of a long and illustrious football career.

Billy kept looking at the clock, and, in his mind, it wasn't moving. He picked it up to see if he could hear it ticking, and it was. If you watch a clock, this tends to happen. So, for Billy, the morning of the game seemed to last longer than any other morning he had ever experienced. It was going far too slowly.

Eventually it was time to go. The doorbell rang, and when he opened it, there standing in front of him was Diego Francesco.

'I thought I could give you and your mama a ride to the ground, if that's OK,' said Diego shyly.

Billy smiled and gave him a huge hug. Diego returned it with one of his own.

'I take it that means yes,' said a smiling Diego.

'Yes, yes, yes,' replied Billy. 'This is going to be the greatest day of my life.'

Every single day was becoming his best day.

The team were sitting quietly, nervously listening to the crowd chanting inside and outside the stadium. When Billy arrived, they looked at him and smiled. Nobody said a word, as they were all fighting a battle to keep their breakfast inside them.

Mr Jenkins walked in and read out the team, with Billy the first name on the list. The excitement of hearing his name erupted inside him. He wanted to jump up and punch the air, but instead said a simple,

'Thank you, sir.'

'Don't let me down,' replied Mr Jenkins.

The bell rang, and the team stood up ready to walk onto the pitch. As they left the changing area, they could see the sunlight reflecting on the beautiful green grass that was the football pitch.

They walked onto the field. Billy thought he was never going to forget seeing it for the first time. It was amazing. Billy looked at the crowd and thought there must have been ten thousand people already in the stadium, ready to watch their game.

He looked up into the seating area and saw his coach sitting next to his mother. Coach had kept his promise and had come to watch him play. Billy wished that he had been able to introduce them. His mum did not know that the person sitting next to her had helped to change his life.

Billy smiled and waved in their direction, and they both waved back. The excitement of finally playing at Valley Park was overwhelming, but he couldn't wait to get started. He knew it was going to be a hard game as the other team, Stafford Academy, had won every game. But they hadn't just won. They had annihilated every team in their league.

Billy wanted to win, to repay his mum for her patience with his football obsession. He wanted to repay his coach for transforming him from a below-average player to the player he was today. He also wanted to repay Mr Jenkins, who had given him the opportunity to play in the final.

He looked for Mr Jenkins, but he wasn't around. He then saw him walking onto the pitch, wiping his mouth after being sick. His nerves because of the game had taken their toll on his digestive system. Then he stopped, felt his stomach, turned, and ran back in the direction he had just come from, as he still felt a bit sick.

Finally, the game kicked off. Things didn't start very well, as Chilford Academy went 1–0 down within the first five minutes, and by half-time they were losing 2–0. The whole team had worked hard, but they were playing against the hardest team they had played in the tournament, and they were not quite ready for the difficulty of the game.

In the second half, the team came out ready for action and played as if they were a completely different team. Billy began to play like the player he had always imagined he would be. He played with confidence, he played with skill, he was able to dribble past players, and it wasn't long before he scored his first goal of the game, from twenty yards out into the bottom left-hand corner.

His name was beamed onto the big screens in the corners of the stadium. The fans began chanting his name, singing,

'Billy Biggs, Billy Biggs.'

Billy stood for a moment and listened, amazed by what he was hearing. It made it even clearer to him, if it wasn't already, that this was what he wanted to do for the rest of his life.

The chanting drove Billy to perform better than he had ever performed before. He crossed the ball into the box and Liberty headed it into the net. The score was now 2–2.

With only injury time left to play, Billy got the ball in his own half and dribbled past two players. He passed the ball to Malcolm, who was running down the left wing, and sprinted into the opposing team's half of the pitch. Malcolm looked up and crossed the ball to the edge of the eighteen-yard box. Billy jumped up into the air, did a 360-degree turn and kicked the ball into the top right-hand corner of the net.

The crowd was stunned into silence. They couldn't believe their eyes. They hadn't seen anything like it before in their lives.

Billy stood up and looked around. Suddenly there was a huge cheer.

'Goal...'

The crowd went wild as they watched the repeat on the big screen. Billy looked over at his mum and Coach. They each had a big smile on their faces, and Coach gave Billy the thumbs up. Billy was congratulated by his teammates, but as he looked up in the direction of his coach again, he was gone.

Coach's seat was immediately taken by another person. His job there was done.

The goalkeeper picked the ball out of the net and kicked it high up into the air in anger. It flew in the direction of Billy's mum. Billy saw it but couldn't do anything about it. His mum saw it heading in her direction but was in too much of a shock to move. It was about to hit her in the face, when suddenly two huge hands reached up and caught the ball. Billy saw that those two big hands belonged to ... Mr Hussain.

The final whistle was blown, and the crowd cheered as Billy lifted the trophy.

Suddenly there was a huge chant from the crowd,

'Sign him up, sign him up, sign him up.'

Billy smiled as he left the pitch, clutching the trophy.

Diego was waiting for him as he entered the dressing room.

'An amazing display, Billy,' Diego said with enthusiasm. 'This is Matty Smith, head of the academy here. He wants to sign you up.'

Billy almost dropped the trophy after hearing the news, but managed to keep his grip on it.

'What do you think?' asked Matty.

'Erm, let me think… Yes, of course.'

'Diego will bring you to see me after the game and we will sign the contract.'

They both left the changing room, and the team celebrated with a nice bottle of cola.

'Well,' said Billy to himself. 'They were all correct after all. Dream big, work hard, and your dreams can come true.'

Lightning Source UK Ltd.
Milton Keynes UK
UKHW021147160721
387271UK00009B/1846

9 781914 083143